"Oh, God. What Hope gasped.

Tristan would have been amused at the panic rounding her violet eyes if he hadn't been wondering the same thing himself.

He rarely acted impulsively. He trusted his instincts, which seldom failed him. But this time his instincts had fully deserted him.

All because of this virginal, violet-eyed temptress.

"What have we done?" he repeated.

The irony burned. A week ago he'd started out thinking he'd like to taste Hope Leoni's soft-looking lips. That was all.

He hadn't gotten a kiss. He hadn't "gotten" anything that everybody in town seemed to think he'd been "getting."

No, he hadn't gotten a kiss....

He'd gotten a wife!

Dear Reader,

During the warm days of July, what better way to kick back and enjoy the best of summer reading than with six stellar stories from Special Edition as we continue to celebrate Silhouette's 20th Anniversary all year long!

With *The Pint-Sized Secret*, Sherryl Woods continues to delight her readers with another winning installment of her popular miniseries AND BABY MAKES THREE: THE DELACOURTS OF TEXAS. Reader favorite Lindsay McKenna starts her new miniseries, MORGAN'S MERCENARIES: MAVERICK HEARTS, with *Man of Passion,* her fiftieth book. A stolen identity leads to true love in Patricia Thayer's compelling *Whose Baby Is This?* And a marriage of convenience proves to be anything but in rising star Allison Leigh's *Married to a Stranger* in her MEN OF THE DOUBLE-C RANCH miniseries. Rounding off the month is celebrated author Pat Warren's *Doctor and the Debutante,* where the healthy dose of romance is just what the physician ordered, while for the heroine in Beth Henderson's *Maternal Instincts*, a baby-sitting assignment turns into a practice run for motherhood—and marriage.

Hope you enjoy this book and the other unforgettable stories Special Edition is happy to bring you this month!

All the best,

Karen Taylor Richman,
Senior Editor

Please address questions and book requests to:
Silhouette Reader Service
U.S.: 3010 Walden Ave., P.O. Box 1325, Buffalo, NY 14269
Canadian: P.O. Box 609, Fort Erie, Ont. L2A 5X3

ALLISON LEIGH
MARRIED TO A STRANGER

Silhouette®

SPECIAL ▼ **EDITION**®

Published by Silhouette Books

America's Publisher of Contemporary Romance

For my daughters.

Live your dreams.

SILHOUETTE BOOKS

ISBN 0-373-24336-7

MARRIED TO A STRANGER

Printed in U.S.A.

ALLISON LEIGH

started early by writing a Halloween play that her grade-school class performed for her school. Since then, though her tastes have changed, her love for reading has not. And her writing appetite simply grows more voracious by the day.

Born in Southern California, she has lived in eight different cities in four different states. She has been, at one time or another, a cosmetologist, a computer programmer and an administrative assistant.

Allison and her husband currently make their home in Arizona, where their time is thoroughly filled with two very active daughters, full-time jobs, pets, church, family and friends. In order to give herself the precious writing time she craves, she burns a lot of midnight oil.

A great believer in the power of love—her parents still hold hands—she cannot imagine anything more exciting to write about than the miracle of two hearts coming together.

Prologue

All he'd wanted was a kiss. A simple kiss.

So how on God's green earth had his life gotten so out of control in just one week over something so simple?

Tris rolled his head against the cushioned seat and looked across the aisle of the custom-fitted jet. Hope was still asleep. She certainly had no head for alcohol.

His jaw was so tight it ached. He had earned himself a doozy of a headache, too. But he knew it wasn't from champagne, or whiskey or anything even remotely alcoholic. He'd barely choked down the few toasts they'd had at the reception—half a glass of champagne wasn't anywhere near enough to set this pain in his head to throbbing.

No, his headache had begun a little over a week ago, he knew. Brought on strictly by himself.

He shoved his fingers through his hair and closed his eyes. But the sight of the woman stretched out on the long seat across from him was firmly burned into his brain.

Hope's toffee-colored hair had fallen loose at some point on the drive to the airport. When he'd carried her onto the private jet, the long, thick waves had clung to his shirt, flowed over his arm and streamed behind them in the night breeze. Now, they lay tangled and gleaming over her shoulders, off the couch, nearly touching the carpeted floor.

He'd slipped off her narrow-heeled shoes and set them on the floor beside her. Her dress—so obviously an antique that he knew women who'd have given their eyeteeth for the ankle-length garment—had worked its way up her shapely calves. With one knee drawn upward, the fabric pulled in a taut stretch of beige-tinted lace over the back of her thighs and her derriere.

She was a total innocent, and lying there, so soundly asleep, she was temptation personified.

Temptation. That's what had gotten them into this mess in the first place. Tris should have known better than to flirt with temptation. God knows *she* didn't have enough experience to fight the blistering sparks between them.

But he was experienced. And older. And he should have known better. His heart might not be programmed for love and happily-ever-after, but he was on a first-name basis with the desires of the flesh.

Tris could feel the plane banking. There was no point in looking out the little oval windows. It was pitch-dark out there. Dark above, dark below, dark all around.

Even this luxurious main cabin of the plane was dark, except for one small lamp burning near him. It cast enough glow to highlight the lace dress and glossy hair of the woman across from him.

He wasn't sure how long he sat there, legs sprawled out before him, his chin resting on his steepled fingers. It could have been one hour or three. But finally, Hope sighed deeply and shifted. Her hand tumbled off the cushion and grazed the carpet. The light glinted on the platinum rings—one plain and one studded with a trio of excruciatingly perfect diamonds—circling her ring finger.

The rings *he* had put there.

She turned her head and pushed her thick hair out of her eyes. She blinked drowsily and he figured her vision was probably blurry, because her eyeglasses were sitting on the round side table beside his seat.

Comprehension slowly dawned in her eyes. He waited, knowing just when that memory clicked into place, because she breathed in sharply and yanked her feet off the cushion to sit up.

"Where are we?" Hope pressed a trembling hand to her head.

"More than halfway to Paris."

Her shoulders seemed to sag. "I drank too much," she murmured. "I've never—*Oh, God.* What have we done?"

Tris would have been amused at the panic rounding her violet eyes if he hadn't been wondering the same thing. He rarely acted impulsively. And even his actions over the last few days had been fairly deliberate. He trusted his instincts, listened to his gut because it rarely failed him.

But now, sitting here in this private jet equipped with every comfort known to man, from a whirlpool tub and a down-covered bed, to a fully equipped kitchen, to an array of computerized equipment that could run a small country if need be, his instincts had fully deserted him.

All because of this violet-eyed temptress.

"What have we done?" he repeated. He'd taken the easiest path of solving her problem. "We've stopped the gossip about us, effectively removing any reason for you to lose your teaching job."

That's *all* they'd done.

The irony burned. He'd started out thinking he'd like to taste her soft-looking lips. That was all.

He still hadn't kissed her. Not really. That quick, off-centered glancing of lips earlier that day didn't count.

He hadn't gotten a kiss. He hadn't "gotten" anything that everybody in town and beyond seemed to think he'd been "getting." It was almost laughable.

Tris picked up her eyeglasses and leaned forward, handing them to her. But in the end, nothing about this situation was laughable.

Particularly the fact that the young woman slipping the gold-rimmed glasses on her nose had—less than twelve hours ago, stood where he'd long ago vowed never to stand—in front of a minister, promising to "love, honor and cherish."

He hadn't gotten a kiss.

He'd gotten a wife.

Chapter One

Eight days earlier.

"**I** think that's plenty, darlin'. If you don't mind."

Hope Leoni blinked, dragged her eyes from the deep blue gaze of the man sitting at the counter across from her. And realized she was pouring coffee all across the counter.

Well, not precisely across the counter. But it was overflowing the thick white coffee cup, the utilitarian saucer beneath it, quickly pooling around the base. Worse, it flowed into a rich brown river that ran straight to the edge of the counter and into the smoky gray sweater the man wore, creating a large spot where he'd been leaning against the counter edge. Now he sat back with a muffled comment.

Her cheeks burned and she hastily set down the glass coffee carafe and grabbed a cloth from behind the counter, mopping up her mess. "I'm so sorry." She mopped, sopped, wiped and tried not to stare when, with a spare movement, he yanked the sweater over his head and tossed it onto the stool beside him. She dragged her attention from the plain white T-shirt that remained, hugging his broad shoulders, only to realize she was equally distracted by the thick gold hair that tumbled over his forehead. "I don't know what I was thinking—"

He, the man...the blond god with a face that could make angels weep...put one hand over hers, stopping her motions. "No sweat, darlin'."

She didn't know which made her blood flow faster until it zipped along her veins with a fevered frenzy—the touch of his hand atop hers, or the casual endearment murmured in his low voice. The schoolgirl fantasies in which he'd been the star seemed as recent as yesterday. "I, uh, I'm not usually so clumsy. I can't believe I—"

"Hey." His long, long fingers encircled hers. Slid around her hand, beneath it; square, warm palm meeting hers. Warm. Dry. Hard.

Every sound faded—the dog that had been barking half the morning from where it was tied up outside the sheriff's office a few doors down, the tractor mower that somebody was running over at the high school, the music from the radio on the shelf in the corner.

All of that faded. She could hear her pulse, thundering in her ears. Could hear her breath, slowly easing past her lips. She could hear the soft chink of his gold wristwatch as it bumped the counter beneath their hands.

"Relax," he said in that voice that hypnotized. "Nobody's going to fire you over a little spilled coffee. Certainly not Ruby, who's got a heart bigger than Wyoming."

At the mention of Ruby, owner of Ruby's Café and, more importantly, Hope's grandmother, some of Hope's scattered senses returned. She tugged her hand, relieved and disappointed all at once when their hands separated. She picked up the damp cloth, rubbing her palm against the wet, rough, terry cloth. "I'm well aware of Gram's generosity."

"Gram?"

Hope pulled her gaze from his mouth. From the way it tilted at the corner when he spoke as if he were perpetually amused. "Ah…Ruby. You know… she's my grandmother. I'm Hope. Hope…Leoni."

He nodded, giving her the impression that he was absorbing every nonsensical syllable she uttered. Which was, of course, ridiculous.

Men who looked like this man didn't hang on every syllable of the very ordinary Hope Leoni. Only he was nodding, his eyes thoughtful. "That's right," he said. "Ruby did have a little granddaughter she was raising."

"I didn't think you'd remember that." Again, she forced herself to look beyond the mesmerizing way his lips shaped his words—to take in the thick, burnished blond hair, the sapphire-colored eyes that even dark circles beneath couldn't dim, the sharply angled jaw. The astounding width of his shoulders.

"You, um, don't visit Weaver very often." Hope felt her cheeks heat all over again.

When he'd moved away from Wyoming, she truly had been Ruby's "little" granddaughter. But that hadn't kept her or any other girl growing up in Weaver from developing a crush on the Wyoming boy who'd made good.

"Well, I'm here now and it's nice to meet you, officially, Hope Leoni. Tristan Clay." He shifted and stuck out his hand, obviously waiting.

Hope swallowed, placing her hand in his. She was almost prepared for the jolt, but still her breath audibly caught and her cheeks burned. "You, too, Mr—ah, Clay."

His smile widened gently but there was something daunting about his impossibly steady gaze, so intensely blue among thick lashes that were surprisingly dark for someone so blond and golden. "Tristan'll do."

She swallowed, far too aware that he still held her hand engulfed in his much larger one. "I suppose you're here for your father's wedding. The whole town is buzzing with excitement."

Finally, finally, his lashes lowered. His thumb brushed across the back of her hand. "This town buzzes with excitement when the lone traffic signal turns red. Do you work here all the time, Hope?"

She knew she should pull away her hand. But his thumb made that gentle little swirl again and she couldn't bring herself to move. "Yes," she breathed. "No. I mean, I work here during the summer. When school starts, I'll—"

His expression didn't change. "School?"

"I teach at the elementary school. Kindergarten through third."

"Lucky kids. Married? Engaged? Going steady?"

She swallowed, nearly choking. "No."

Again that smooth, gentle swirl against her hand, the faint tilt at the corner of his mouth. "Why not?"

Her fingers curved. She tugged again and had the impression that he wanted to smile when she pushed her hands into the front pockets of her pink waitress uniform. "No particular reason," she answered, hoping that her trembling nerves didn't show in her voice as badly as she suspected. Except she'd have to be asked on a date again before she could worry about marriage proposals. "You?" His smile widened a bit, and he shook his head. Her cheeks flamed hotly. Of course, in a town as small as Weaver, news would have spread like wildfire if he had settled down with one woman.

He was Tristan Clay, the youngest of the Clay brothers of the enormous Double-C cattle ranch located some twenty miles away from town. He was rich, golden-beautiful and successful even without his family's holdings, which were reportedly the largest in the state. He'd developed some type of software when he'd been younger than she was now that had revolutionized the industry. Had dated famous women, danced in Europe with princesses and slept in the White House.

When Hope had been in school, every girl in town had dreamed of capturing the interest of Tristan Clay on his rare visits to his family's ranch. It didn't matter that he was grown and gone and the schoolgirls were just that—girls. The articles about him in the newspapers or magazines years ago had been clipped, savored in scrapbooks or tacked up on bedroom walls.

Hope had so envied her friend, Jolie, who had been allowed to pin up her favorite articles about her latest heartthrob. Gram had refused to let Hope attach anything to her bedroom walls other than a landscape or a print of the Last Supper. As if by doing so she'd be able to prevent Hope from turning into the wild child her sister Justine had been.

But Gram hadn't known about the clipping Hope had had inside her geometry book. The one of Tristan, when he'd made the papers about some high-tech espionage he'd foiled. His appearances in the news had dwindled to nothing over the last six or seven years—a fact that had roused its own share of curiosity—but Hope knew, to her everlasting embarrassment, that her private hoard of clippings were still packed away somewhere in her closet.

And now, here *he* sat, across the counter from where she stood, with his intense blue gaze steady on her face as if there was no place else in the world he wanted to be.

Ridiculous, of course. Tristan Clay was just killing time until he headed out to his family's place.

Yet, he *was* here in her grandmother's café, wearing blue jeans that were washed soft and nearly white. The dark gray crew-neck sweater he'd worn had looked like cashmere. But he'd dumped it on the stool with no regard for the coffee soaking it. And if she wasn't mistaken, there'd even been a small hole in one of the cuffs that had been pushed halfway up his golden-brown, sinewy forearms.

For a self-professed computer geek, his body looked both lean and hard. Her cheeks heated once again at her wayward thoughts. Since when did she speculate on the hardness of a man's body? *Not since you were a silly teenager, mooning over an article clipping about a man completely out of your league.*

Now her ears were burning, too. She swiped a loose strand of hair away from her cheek, nudged up the nose piece of her glasses and made a production of looking at the round clock high on the wall at the end of the counter.

It was three-thirty and the café was supposed to close at two every day until it reopened at six. But Hope had left the front and back doors propped open to take advantage of the lovely June afternoon while she prepared for the supper crowd.

It wasn't the first summer she'd spent working in her grandmother's café. It wasn't likely to be the last. But come the fall, Hope would begin her second year of teaching at Weaver Elementary and her mind had been filled with plans of that. And the relief of it, because she'd known the vote of the three-person school board to keep the school open at all had been terribly close.

She'd come out of the kitchen, her head filled with school projects and ideas, only to find Tristan sitting at one of the counter stools. His arms had been folded across the shining surface, his wide shoulders hunched tiredly. She'd begun telling him they were closed, but he'd looked up and Hope had been lost in the intensity of his eyes.

Tristan had been gone from the area for so long

that he probably didn't remember that Ruby's Café closed after lunch. Yet telling him that was quite possibly the last thing on this earth that she'd wanted to do.

She now cast around for something intelligent to say. But could only think of the same topic she'd brought up earlier. "So, you're here for your father's wedding next Saturday?"

He nodded and shifted on the stool, finally blinking his eyes and glancing away. But only for a moment. One moment when she could breathe normally, and then he looked at her again, and she simply forgot how. She nudged at her slipping glasses, then pushed her hands into her pockets once more. "I've met Gloria Day." She felt the tips of her ears go hot at the way the words seemed to blurt out of her. "She's very nice. I, uh, hope your father and she are very happy."

He nodded, not replying. His long fingers wrapped around the cup and he tilted it, as if to drink. Hope automatically reached for the coffee pot and refilled his cup. "Did you want to see a menu?" She ignored the fact that she was due at her friend's house in less than ten minutes. She'd promised to watch Evan, Jolie's son, while Jolie and Drew Taggart drove to Gillette.

"I remember when Ruby used to just write the specials on that chalkboard over there." Tristan glanced at the square board that was propped on a high corner shelf.

"She still puts the specials on the board." Hope pulled a menu from beneath the counter and slid it across to him. "But we offer more these days. I could fix you a sandwich or something."

"Coffee, tea or me?" Tris wanted to retract the suggestive words as soon as he said them. But they were already out there and hectic color was staining the waitress-teacher's cheeks. Personally, he found the blush charming. How many women did he know anymore who blushed?

But he'd obviously embarrassed her.

"No. I guess not." He was oddly disappointed. She wasn't at all his type of woman. Hell, she looked barely old enough to vote, much less be a teacher. Besides, the only energy he had right now was expended simply by lifting the coffee cup to drain it of its life-giving liquid. He set the empty cup down, closed the menu and pushed to his feet, dropping a few bills on the counter as he did so.

He wondered when he'd become so jaded that he couldn't recognize a naive girl when he met one. Not that he expected to see her again. He had a week to catch up on his brothers' lives, then there was the wedding to get through. After that, he was due to meet Dom to finish up the case that had kept them all occupied far longer than anyone had expected, thanks to the mess made by a love-sick fool on their very own team. He didn't have time to dwell on Hope's innocent appeal. "Thanks for the java." He headed to the open door. "It was just what I needed."

"You're quite welcome."

He looked back at her painfully polite words. Her ivory cheeks were nearly as pink as the uniform-dress thing she wore. Behind her gold-rimmed glasses, her eyes were wide and so violet they looked like crushed flowers from the lilac bushes that bloomed around the big house at the ranch. If it weren't for the glasses, he'd have figured that she was wearing some colored contact lenses to achieve that vivid color. But they were obviously the genuine article.

He cupped his hand tightly around the metal edge of the glass door as his attention drifted from her eyes to the rosy fullness of her lips. To the gentle, rounded curve of her jaw and the smooth line of her throat where the delicate links of a fine gold chain disappeared beneath the ill-fitting uniform. Behind him, a dog barked and he reeled in thoughts that could get him arrested in some states. Apparently, he wasn't as beat from the last week as he'd thought.

"Give my regards to your grandmother."

"I will." Her tongue peeped out, leaving a distracting glisten on her lower lip. "It was nice meeting you."

"You too. Hope."

The color in her cheeks flared again, but she smiled. And he found himself smiling back.

Then he heard his name being called, and turned to see his oldest brother, Sawyer, standing on the street a few yards down. He absently waved at his brother, still looking back inside the café. Feeling disappointed that Hope had turned away, busy with something at the counter.

"Thought you were coming in next week."

Realizing that he was wondering how far her toffee-brown hair would reach down her back if it weren't twisted into that thick, roping braid, Tris deliberately stepped away from the doorway toward Sawyer. Okay, so he took one more look into the café before he did. What was the harm in looking? He was a man. She was a woman.

And his brother was the law now. Tris felt a smile growing on his face as his brother walked closer. The only indication of Sawyer's new status as the sheriff was the star fastened unobtrusively to his leather belt. Except for the billed cap with a naval insignia that he wore, Sawyer looked much the same as the other men in the small rural town he now served. Well-worn blue jeans and a work shirt. "I was," Tris finally answered with a grin. "You're missing the Stetson and spurs."

Sawyer shrugged, tucking the bow of his dark sunglasses in the collar of his shirt. "Left the spurs at home. Rebecca likes 'em, you know," he said blandly.

Tris chuckled. "You wish. How is my newest doctor-in-law?"

"My wife is beautiful and totally in love with me. You can save your charms for someone else." Sawyer leaned his back against the hood of a pickup parked at the curb. "You're early."

"So you already mentioned." Tris looked back toward the café when he heard the soft jingle of a bell. All he saw, though, was the door closing. The blinds had been drawn across all the windows. "Cafe still closed during the afternoons?"

"Regular as rain."

"She didn't tell me," he murmured.

"Ruby?"

"Hope." He felt his brother's look. "What?"

Sawyer just shook his head. "What do you do? Some kind of chant that brings women running?"

"All I had was a cup of coffee." Ordinarily, Tris would have shrugged off his brother's taunt without feeling a shred of defensiveness.

"Yeah, well, I know you. Hope teaches at the elementary school. Everyone in this town looks on her as their daughter, or their sister. So keep your mitts off."

The fact that his brother seemed to think he needed the warning burned. "Thanks for the enthusiastic welcome home, bro."

Sawyer's expression didn't change. Because he was the oldest of his brothers? Because he was the sheriff? Because he was one of Squire Clay's sons and had picked up an endless amount of Clay nosiness along the way?

"Hope Leoni is," *sweet, unbearably sexy and way too innocent,* "of no interest to me," Tris said dismissively. Maybe if he said it with enough conviction, he'd make it true.

Hope's fingers crushed the paper bag holding the rolls she was taking out to the Taggarts, when she heard Tristan's voice, easily carried around the side of the café on the warm summer breeze.

She yanked open the door of her little green car and tossed the sack onto the passenger seat. "Of course you're of no interest to him," she muttered under her breath. She tossed her braid over her shoulder and pushed the key into the ignition, starting the engine with a roar. She threw it into gear and zipped around the side of the café, jouncing out onto Main.

In her rearview mirror she could see Tristan and the sheriff standing on the sidewalk talking. "Men like Tristan Clay don't have interest in women like you." Men in general don't have interest in you. Most of the town still considered her Ruby's "little" granddaughter.

She was a fully qualified teacher. She'd moved into her own house and, despite the barely hidden reluctance of the school board, obtained the teaching position at Weaver Elementary. She didn't know what was worse—still being thought of as a teenager, or knowing that every move she made was measured and compared against the actions of her mother who'd had the temerity to be an unwed mother, twice, or her sister, who'd had to leave high school because of her wild ways.

Maybe she should accept the next time Larry Pope asked her out. He wasn't a bad guy, after all. In fact, as the math teacher at the high school, he was respected and well liked. Maybe if she dated him a time or two, the town would see that she *wasn't* her mother or her sister.

But surely that wasn't a good enough reason to go out with a man? To prove she could date without bringing shame to her grandmother the way people seemed to believe her mother and sister had? Larry was nice, yes. He just didn't make her forget her own name when she looked into his…his…what color *were* Larry's eyes? Whatever color they were, they weren't the deep blue that Tristan Clay's were.

She made an impatient sound. Yes. The next time

Larry Pope asked her out, she'd accept. It wasn't as if there was a line of men beating down her door. It wasn't as if she was ''of interest'' to any male other than Larry Pope.

She hit the brakes abruptly, nearly passing the turn-off to the Taggarts' place.

Several minutes later, she pulled up in front of the partially completed log home that her friends were building. As soon as she stopped the car, the door flew open and Evan tumbled out, racing toward her. ''Auntie Hope,'' he squealed, launching his five-year-old self with considerable enthusiasm at her legs. Hope laughed, swinging the boy in a circle, before settling him back on his feet.

He beamed, gap-toothed, back at her. There was another male who was interested in her after all, Hope thought wryly. Only he was seventeen years her junior and had a seven o'clock bedtime. ''Come on, you,'' she said cheerfully. ''Let's hustle your folks along so we can finish writing your surprise story for your mom's birthday.''

And maybe, while they were at it, she could rid herself of foolish thoughts about Tristan Clay.

Chapter Two

"Here. Hang these bows from the banister there."

Tris heaved a sigh and lowered his arm that he'd laid across his eyes in a vain attempt to block out the light. "I didn't think it possible, but marriage has actually made you *more* bossy," he complained, looking up at his sister-in-law, Emily Clay. She'd been raised with Tris and his brothers after her parents had been killed when she was little. But she'd legally become a Clay when she'd married his brother, Jefferson. And now they even had two kids.

"And time has only made you more lazy. Move it." Emily nudged him with her foot. "What *are* you doing lying here in the living room on the floor, anyway?"

"*Trying* to sleep," he muttered. "So stop sticking your foot in my ribs."

She crouched down beside him, propping her arms on her knees. Her long brown hair slid over her shoulder, rich and dark as coffee. A thought which immediately brought to mind Hope Leoni of the pink cheeks and sweet smile. He squelched a groan and concentrated on Emily, who was speaking to him, her eyebrows raised with curiosity. "You're *trying* to sleep on the floor here in the living room because…?"

"The couch is hard as a rock." He yawned and dropped his arm over his face again. "And because Gloria's daughters are using the guest suite downstairs."

"What about your old bedroom upstairs?"

"Full up with packing boxes from Gloria's house. I'm told they were going to be gone by the time I was expected to arrive next week, but I have my doubts."

"The couch in Matthew's office?"

"Too short. And the rec room downstairs has paper doves and bells on every surface." He flexed his fingers. "Doves, for God's sake."

"It's for a wedding shower, ding dong. You *could* have stayed with Jefferson and me, you know. We've got room, even for a big dope like you."

Tris knew that. He also knew that he could have bunked with Daniel or Sawyer, too. But staying at the main house of the ranch, the "big house," as they all called it, had seemed the easiest choice. Whether or not his father ever said so, Tris knew that staying at the big house was what Squire expected. Available bed or not.

He sat up, rubbing a hand across his jaw. He needed a shave. He'd stayed at Sawyer and Rebecca's place in town until nearly midnight. "What time is it? Where's Squire?"

"Nearly two in the afternoon and he better be in town visiting the barber. Jaimie says you came in late last night, crashed out here and haven't risen since. Hung over?"

"Listen runt, I haven't had a hangover in a month of Sundays." Hell, he rarely drank more than an occasional beer anymore. His days of excess had long passed.

"Then what? You sick?"

"No," he said tolerantly. Em had been his best friend since they were bitty, so he made allowances for her that he ordinarily wouldn't have. "Sleepy. It's not a crime, last I checked."

Her pansy-brown eyes narrowed. "I also heard you've been circling Hope Leoni. She's a little—"

His "allowances" only went so far. "I don't go around jumping the town virgins," he said abruptly. "You know, if my love life was as *active* as everyone seems to think, I'd never get any work done."

"And that work is…?" Her expression softened and she smiled peaceably. "Never mind. I learned just how close-mouthed you Hollins-Winword dudes are from my darling husband. Now, about these bows."

Tris shook his head. "No wonder Jefferson finally succumbed to you. You're worse than water torture."

Her eyes danced. "That's right. And only because I love you will I warn you that the dove-decorated shower is set to begin in less than an hour. There'll be about twenty-five women trooping through this house, and I really don't want to explain your presence on the floor. Might ruin your classy image."

Tris made a face, but rolled to his feet. He rubbed Emily's head, deliberately messing up her hair the way he'd done when they were kids, and headed upstairs, grabbing his duffel from where it still sat inside the dining room doorway.

He'd take a shower, then dive into a gallon of coffee. *Then* he'd consider hanging damned bows from the banister for his sister-in-law. Maybe.

Only, when he came out of the shower, considerably more alert and marginally more presentable in clean jeans and shirt, he could hear a horde of women chattering and laughing as they arrived. If he wanted coffee, he had to go down there among all of them to get it.

Not that he was ever averse to being among women. As far as Tris was concerned, it was one of the more pleasurable places to be. But this was a *wedding* shower.

Frankly, the whole notion made his skin itch.

He waited an interminable twenty caffeine-deprived minutes before he went downstairs to the now-empty kitchen, and the coffee pot that he prayed would be hot and full, as usual.

It was, and he stood there at the counter, singeing his tongue as he downed two fast cups, frowning at the playpen that sat on the floor on the other side of the table next to the wall. For now, it was empty of babies even though the family was full of them these days. Emily, Jaimie and Maggie had all had a baby within the last six months.

He shuddered, poured a third cup of coffee and carried it with him through the mudroom and outside.

The sun was bright. Warm. The air filled with the rich scent of mown grass. Across the gravel road separating the big house from the outbuildings and corrals, horses grazed and Matthew's retriever chased a butterfly.

He squinted and poured more coffee down his throat. He was glad his brothers were busy with the hundred chores required every day to keep the place running. It meant that they were thoroughly busy, and Tris could find another place to grab a few more z's, undisturbed.

He slowly wandered around the side of the house, past lilac bushes heavy with blossoms and immediately thought of Hope's striking eyes. He stifled an oath. He'd learned a lot about Miss Hope Leoni while he'd been hanging out at Sawyer's place the evening before. She was a paragon of virtue; an apparent candidate for sainthood.

Which meant the vivid dream he'd had about her that had awakened him around two in the morning was even more ill-advised.

He went up the front steps of the wide porch. Sighing with anticipation, he lowered himself onto the swing, propped his feet on the railing across from him, and dropped his head onto the wooden swing back.

Oh yeah. This was it. He yawned, scratched his

jaw, and closed his eyes. This was the kind of break he needed. No noise, no tourists, no unexpected disasters at work. No wedding nonsense.

No damned dreams about innocent school teachers with violet eyes.

"Shhh."

"Is he sleeping or is he dead?"

"His feet are *big*. They're even bigger than Daddy's, and I can put *both* my feet in his boot!"

"Girls, quiet down. You'll wake him."

"Do we have to share our juice with him? I don't think we have enough for him. My mommy says Unca Twistin has a 'normous appa...appa—"

"Appetite."

"Yeah. That."

"I'm sure he doesn't want any juice. Come on now, we're going to have our picnic over there by those three trees. Remember?"

"But what if he *does* want some?"

"If he does, we'll share with him. It would be impolite not to."

"But—"

"Sshh. Over to the trees before we wake him."

Tris gritted his teeth, staring at the group of little girls, and one big girl through slitted eyes. "Too late."

The little girls, his nieces, jumped and scattered as if he'd grown three heads. The big girl, however, nudged up her gold-rimmed glasses and blinked with dismay. "I'm sorry. I didn't expect you to be out here sleeping, or I'd have talked the girls into having our picnic elsewhere."

His coffee was cold. He finished it off, anyway, then pulled his feet off the rail and sat forward. "I didn't expect to see you here, either."

Hope moistened her lips. "Well. Sorry to have wakened you." She hefted her caramel-colored wicker basket more firmly between her arms.

He was wakened all right. "What are you doing here?"

"Having a picnic with the girls."

"No, I mean why are you with the kids and not at Gloria's shower?"

"I'm watching the children. Well, these guys, anyway. The babies are with their moms."

"Why are you doing this?"

"Because I was asked to." She shook her head as if the answer was obvious.

"How old are you, Hope?"

She looked over her shoulder at the children who were crossing the gravel drive toward the grass on the other side. "Nearly twenty-three. Sarah, honey, wait until you get to the grass before you take off your shoes," she called.

Nearly twenty-three. Hell. How many women did he know who claimed to be nearly any age but one at least a decade younger than was true? And now he had the hots for the babysitter. *Had* he ever had a babysitter? He tried to remember. Couldn't. Not enough coffee in him yet.

"I'll watch the girls," he said abruptly. They were sweet little things, and he liked playing the uncle. It was as close a relationship to kids as he intended to get. "You go join the women," he finished telling Hope.

"I'm hardly dressed for a wedding shower."

Which only brought his attention to the golden length of calf she displayed below the fringe of her knee-length, cut-off blue jeans. He'd have remembered if he'd ever had a babysitter with legs like that.

"Go on back and go to sleep," she was saying, and he dragged his attention upward, over denim worn thin and...did she have to wear such a baggy T-shirt? The obnoxious lime-green cotton hung around her hips, frustratingly loose and boxy. *The babysitter,* for cryin' out loud!

"But, um, thank you for the offer anyway." She smiled shyly and turned to follow the children.

He gave himself a mental shake. Sleep. That's what he needed. Then he wouldn't feel so...hell, what did he feel? Off balance?

He yawned again, watching the graceful sway of her long braid as she walked away, joining the children.

J.D. and Angeline belonged to Daniel and Maggie. Leandra was Jefferson and Emily's. And Sarah, the youngest, was Matthew and Jaimie's. They all circled around Hope as she joined them and set them to work, spreading a bright yellow sheet.

He smiled faintly, though, when the girls didn't dig into the feast—they were too far away for him to see exactly what it was. But he recognized what the little girls preferred over the food when dozens and dozens of small, opalescent bubbles started floating over their heads, bobbing, swaying, popping.

Even Hope was blowing bubbles. He rested his

arms on the rail and watched her purse her lips, blow and set a wiggling, wobbling train of soap bubbles into the afternoon breeze. She certainly wasn't shy when she dealt with the children.

He narrowed his eyes and pictured her face should he follow them. She'd probably stare at his feet or his left ear, and she'd turn white, then red. And all the while he'd be thinking he'd like to see her when she wasn't wearing that baggy T-shirt that hid her curves from prying eyes like his.

God. He sat back in his chair and pressed the heels of his palms against his eye sockets. He was every bit the lech that his family seemed to think he was.

But even that knowledge didn't take him back inside the house. No, he propped his feet back on the rail and continued watching Hope. If the way she kept sneaking looks back toward the house now and again was any indication, she was doing some of her own watching, too.

"I thought I saw you driving a green car yesterday."

Hope whirled around at the voice behind her. She was waiting in the kitchen of the ranch house for her ride back to Weaver. By the time she'd shepherded the girls back to the big house, the shower guests had departed. That's what she got for letting the little ones talk her into walking all over creation—and the Double-C had plenty of interesting places to explore.

Now, Tristan was looking at her with his incredible eyes, waiting for an answer and she wished, cowardly, that the children were still with her instead of their parents.

"Yes, I have a car," she admitted. "But I rode out here with Dr. Rebecca."

"And where is Dr. Rebecca now?"

Hope curled her fingers over the back of one of the chairs at the enormous oval table that sat in the center of the big kitchen. "She was called away on a house call."

"So you need a ride home, then."

"Jaimie is going to drive me."

"Jaimie drives like a bat out of hell. I'll take you."

Hope's stomach jolted. He was far more harmless when he was sleeping. When he was wide awake and watching her from beneath heavy lids, he was totally devastating. Totally daunting. Why would he offer to drive her? It wasn't as if she was "of interest" to him. "Jaimie has already offered."

"You really prefer to ride with the speed demon?"

Hope swallowed. "I—"

"Stop tormenting our guest," Jaimie chided sailing into the kitchen and poking her brother-in-law in the back. "And I haven't gotten a speeding ticket in months."

"That's 'cause your daughter calls the sheriff *uncle,*" Tris countered dryly. "I want to go by and see Drew Taggart anyway. There's no point in all of us driving into town."

Hope folded her hands together and wished she'd driven herself. But Jaimie looked her way, eyebrows lifting. And Hope forced herself to shrug as if it didn't matter in the least how she got back home.

So she found herself sitting beside him in the close confines of his rental car as he drove along the gravel drive toward the main gate of his family's ranch. With each vibrating turn of the tires, Hope felt herself growing more uncomfortable. She was wrinkled and sweaty and her unmanageable hair was working loose from its ordinarily tidy braid. He, on the other hand, made his faded jeans seem like a sinful sight; and she swore she could still smell the freshness of his shower on that golden skin.

She stared out the window and banished thoughts of Tristan and showers.

He hadn't turned on the radio. It was just the two of them and the sound of the tires. And Hope felt more tongue-tied than she'd ever felt in her life.

Considering she'd spent most of her life tongue-tied, that was quite a feat.

"Would you like to grab some dinner?"

She turned and looked at him, her lips parting soundlessly.

"Is that a yes or a no?"

He wasn't asking her for dinner. He couldn't be. Why *would* he? He was only driving her home because he'd been going by to see Drew anyway. "I don't…ah, no. Thank you."

"Why?"

She stared fixedly out at the passing landscape. "Excuse me?"

"Why won't you have dinner with me? We could grab a steak at Colbys."

"Why?" She glanced at him long enough to see the corner of his lips deepen.

"That was my question."

She folded her arms. She didn't like being teased. "I have plans."

"Big date?"

Her cheeks burned. "Is that so hard to believe?"

He smiled faintly. "Not at all."

It ought to be, she thought silently. The last time Hope had been on a date, she'd still been in college. And she may have entertained thoughts of agreeing if Larry Pope asked her out again, but that occasion hadn't actually occurred. "I have to wash my hair."

He raised his eyebrows. "In other words, you're not interested."

"No," she blurted. "I mean, I...I do have to wash my hair. Church is tomorrow."

His smile widened wryly. "Naturally. It's been a while since I've been thrown over for shampoo and conditioner."

Hope closed her eyes and wished for the drive to be over.

When they finally entered the official outskirts of town, Hope started to tell him where she lived, but without any prompting at all, he drove straight to the cozy little house she rented across the street from the park and the high school.

"Sawyer told me," he said, as he parked in her narrow driveway.

Hope shoved open the car door, just glad to be home and certainly not willing to wonder why Tristan and his brother had even discussed the where-abouts of her home, but Tristan caught her arm before she could escape. Her throat tightened and she looked over her shoulder at him. "I appreciate the ride."

Because he couldn't help himself, Tris looked into her eyes.

They were the purest violet he'd ever seen, so dark he could barely distinguish the pupil from the iris. And the whites were whiter than any white that had ever existed. Annoyance and amazement churned inside him. A few days' dalliance with this girl-woman was out of the question. He knew it. So why did he ask her for dinner? And why did it bug him to his core that she'd refused? "Eyes as clear as yours just don't exist," he murmured.

Her eyebrows popped up. "Excuse me?"

"I'll bet you've never had a hangover. Never crossed the street against the light. Never stayed up later than you should."

Color suffused her cheeks. "I *have* been to college."

"Sweet pea, compared to the places I've been, that doesn't mean diddly." His voice lowered. "Never had an impure thought."

Her eyes flickered and she hurriedly climbed from the car. Her thick braid bounced in counterpoint to her hasty steps as she walked away from him.

Let her go.

He swallowed an oath along with the common sense that told him to leave well enough alone. He caught up to her as she pushed open the front door of her little white house. The place was as neat and tidy as she was, with precise rows of summer flowers in the beds lining the sidewalk. He closed his hand around her elbow, pulling her up short before she could shut the door in his face.

"Wait."

Her chin tilted, but her eyes wouldn't meet his.

"Why? So you can make fun of me some more?"

"I wasn't."

She didn't answer. The way her soft lips twisted was answer enough.

He frowned. The bones in her elbow felt fragile. He slid his hand up her arm, curving around the taut flesh, feeling the flex of healthy muscle. Of skin that was smooth as satin against his fingertips. "I have to go back to Paris after the wedding."

She blinked. Hesitated. "Congratulations."

"It's business," he dismissed. "I travel a lot." Too much, he thought vaguely. "I'm not going to be here for long. Why won't you have dinner with me? I'm harmless."

Hope's lips parted and she looked down at his fingers circling her arm. Harmless? Hardly. This man was built for harm. Harm of the heart. "I don't—"

"Want steak. That's okay. Pizza, then."

"Why are you doing this?"

"Man's gotta eat." He didn't smile. "Woman's gotta eat, too. What's your favorite food?"

She frowned. "Chinese. I don't—"

"We'd have to drive a ways to get that."

His thumb swirled against her arm. She looked up at him. "Tristan—"

"Maybe I like the way you say my name."

Her throat knotted. Shivers crept down her spine and broke out on her arm where he would surely feel them. He probably thought she was insane standing there shivering in the warm early evening. "I'm a mess from this afternoon," she whispered thoughtlessly.

Tris looked at her lips. They were perfectly sculpted, impossibly soft-looking. Everything about her was soft. Her voice, her eyes, her skin. "Take a shower," he murmured. "I'll wash your back." He wasn't entirely joking, he realized. But he grinned, trying to look harmless despite his thoughts which were miles away from harmless.

"Colbys," she said abruptly, tugging her arm out of his grasp. "It'll be a zoo at the pizza place. I'll meet you there in a half hour." Then she hastily stepped into the house and shut the door right in his face.

Tris stared at the closed door. "I'll be damned," he murmured. Then he laughed softly, feeling better than he had in weeks, and turned around on her postage-stamp-sized porch. Across the street, the park stretched out, vibrantly green. The high school looked the same as always. And down the street and around the corner was the old elementary school. Where, among her students, shy Hope would laugh and smile and teach.

Too bad he'd be long gone from Weaver by then. He'd have enjoyed seeing Hope in her element.

He'd just have to figure a way in the next few days to get her to look him in the eye with those incredible eyes of hers. To scale that mile-high shyness of hers so that when he kissed her—he wasn't sure when he'd decided it was something he *was* going to do—she wouldn't run away.

She'd kiss him back.

The kiss was definitely something he looked forward to. Probably more than was good for either of them. But it would be *just* a kiss. What would be the harm in that?

Chapter Three

"Would you like wine?"

Beneath the cover of the varnished wood table top, Hope's fingers twisted together. "No, thank you." She didn't drink. Hadn't ever had a hangover, just as he'd said earlier.

She watched Tristan, who sat across from her in the dimly lit booth. He showed no surprise that she'd declined the drink. Of course he wasn't surprised.

The only surprise was that she was sitting here in Colbys, which served food but which everyone still considered a bar, with Tristan Clay. Hope had been to Colbys dozens of times in her lifetime. Never once had the booths seemed so cramped. So shadowy. So intimate.

Tristan was reading the menu he held open between his hands. His fingers idly tapped the corner of the padded vinyl folder and Hope closed her eyes for a moment before focusing on her own menu. She shifted and her knee bumped something solid and immovable beneath the table. It wasn't the table. It was him. She quickly angled her knees away from his and stared blindly at the menu. What was she doing here?

"Decided yet?"

She looked up as Tristan closed his menu and sat back in the booth. "Excuse me?"

His eyebrow peaked. "Do you know what you want to order?"

She nodded and shut her menu with a snap. She didn't. But she wasn't going to sit there like an idiot staring at words that her distracted mind wouldn't read. She chewed at the inside of her lip. Rearranged her flatware and drained her water glass.

He closed the menu and set it to the side of the table, folding his arms over the surface of the table. He seemed suddenly to loom over her from his side, but the portion of her brain that still functioned knew it only seemed that way because he was so tall and his shoulders so wide that he easily filled more than half of the bench on his side of the booth.

A fact that did nothing to prevent her from pressing her spine more firmly against the seat behind her. Or from reaching for the chain at her throat and running an inch of it back and forth between her thumb and forefinger.

His gaze was unwavering, but she was certain that he wanted to smile. She felt her entire body go hot with embarrassment. She dropped her hand to her lap.

She wished that Newt Rasmusson, the owner of the place, would hurry up and take their orders—despite the fact that she didn't know what she wanted—so at least that interruption would draw Tristan's focus away from her.

"Want to dance?"

The jangle that shot through her was *not* a leaping, internal YES! It simply wasn't. "No one is dancing," she pointed out faintly. Her fingers sought the chain necklace once again.

"So?"

"There's no music."

He glanced down at the table. "If you don't want to, Hope, just say so."

"I didn't mean—"

His lashes lifted and she saw, then, the amusement there. Her lips tightened and she angled her chin up a notch. She gathered up her purse and started to slide from the bench. No matter how breathless she became just from looking at him, she wasn't going to sit there and be his evening's entertainment. He'd already found more than enough about her to tease. "This was a bad idea," she said aloud. Her voice shook, but at least she'd spoken up. "Thank you for the ride back to town earlier."

Without looking his way, she hurried toward the entrance, bumping her hip against an empty table as she went. She tugged the strap of her shoulder bag higher on her shoulder and blinked rapidly. She pushed through the door, nearly crying with relief when she made it out onto the street without embarrassing herself even more than she already had.

Though how that would be possible, she couldn't

be sure. "Idiot," she muttered under her breath. She drew in a long breath and started down the street in the direction of her house. It wouldn't take but a few minutes to walk. No longer than it would have taken her to walk *to* Colbys in the first place if Tristan hadn't been sitting on her little porch when she came out, ready to drive them despite her assertion that she'd meet him there.

"I guess you weren't hungry, after all."

She whirled, her braid flying. Her lips parted, but no words came. And that frustrated her even more. She shook her head and turned again, but Tristan caught her arm. His fingers circled her elbow; not tightly, but with enough insistence that she stopped again. Or maybe it was the tingling heat spreading out from her elbow along the rest of her arm. Her voice broke free. "Tristan, don't."

He stepped in front of her, oblivious to the two cars that slowly drove down the main street. His shoulders blocked the red glow of the setting sun. "Am I so objectionable that you couldn't stand one more minute of my company?"

Her fingers curled around her purse strap. "I don't like being laughed at."

"Nobody does, sweet pea." He let go of her elbow and brushed his thumb over her white knuckles. "The only one I was laughing at was myself," he said quietly. "Please. Come back in and have dinner with me. I won't ask you to dance if you don't want me to, but I can't promise not to try talking you into a game of pool."

She didn't want to be charmed by him, knowing how easily he could accomplish it. *Was* accomplishing it. "What about Drew Taggart?" she asked, faintly desperate.

"What about him?"

"You wanted to look him up."

"I'll catch up to him later. There's plenty of time."

"But you told Jaimie—"

"You'd have been racing down the road with her at the wheel if I'd just told you, flat out, what my reasons were for offering you that ride."

He didn't wear boots like most of the men in Weaver did. Not cowboy boots nor heavy work boots. He wore scuffed athletic shoes. She stared at them so fiercely that she spotted the tiny place at the toe of one shoe where the leather had begun to wear through. "And what were they? These reasons that would terrify me so?"

"I'll tell you, but you have to look at me first."

Her cheeks heated. She darted a look into his face.

He tsked, and she jumped when he tucked his knuckles under her chin and lifted it. Nervousness knotted in her chest. "I'm looking at you."

"At my chin," he murmured. He touched the nose piece of her glasses, inching them back up her nose, and surprise lifted her gaze to his for the briefest of moments.

But it was long enough for her to be caught, unable to pull her gaze from his. They were so blue, his eyes. As if a midnight sky had been trapped in his irises. She suddenly felt warm, her senses trapped in some odd time warp where everything moved slowly. She didn't even blink when he took a step closer, wrapping his other hand around her free elbow. Her hands brushed his hips and she pulled them back, clasping them together against her chest.

"That's why," he murmured.

His thumb was doing that maddening swirl-thing on her elbow. "I d-don't know."

"Yes, you do, Hope."

"No—"

"Don't be afraid of me."

"I'm…not." She swallowed. "I'm not."

"You're trembling."

"I—"

"So am I."

"Stop this. You're making fun. You told your brother you weren't interested in me. I overheard you."

"I'm interested all right," he murmured.

She shook her head abruptly. Her protest was as ineffectual as her mushy resistance when he drew his fingertips along her forearms, capturing her hands. He pressed her palms to his chest. And, oh God, she felt his heart. Thundering through the fine cotton of his Hawaiian print shirt as fiercely as her own heart pounded.

"You're doing that to me, sweet pea." His soft words stirred the loose tendrils of hair at her temples. "You have been since the coffee in the café. Maybe I didn't see that it was any of my brother's business, but that doesn't mean it's not so."

"No."

"Yes. That's why I was laughing at myself. I come home expecting nothing but enduring my old man's long-awaited wedding, and find myself meeting a teacher whose violet eyes could make me forget my own name.''

She felt his breath on her forehead, then closed her eyes and held back a gasp when his warm lips touched her temple. Her fingers curled against his chest, grabbing loose fabric. ''We're standing on Main Street.''

His jaw grazed hers, then he lifted his head, untangling her fingers from his shirt front. ''If it bothers you, come back inside with me and have dinner.''

''You said you were harmless. I knew you were lying.'' She frowned as another car pulled along the street and turned into the parking lot behind her. ''What do you want with me?''

He laughed abruptly. ''Are you kidding?''

''You used to date Serena Stevenson.'' She pushed out the words.

His eyes narrowed. ''So? It was a long time ago.''

''She's a famous model!''

''Who is now happily married with two kids, neither of whom are mine, thank the good Lord. What's your point?''

''My face has never stopped traffic.''

''That's because you've probably always been in Weaver where there *is* no traffic.'' He let go of her hands and took a step back. The cool fingers of the evening air slipped between them and Hope shivered.

She hadn't always been in Weaver and she knew good and well that guys who looked this good didn't seek out Hope Leoni because of her physical attributes. Only she couldn't for the life of her think what Tristan hoped to gain by pursuing this.

Which brought her squarely back to the assumption that he was merely amusing himself. His heart may have seemed to thunder in tempo with hers. But in all likelihood it had just been her muddled senses. Which were quickly clearing again, thank goodness.

"I think you should go see Drew," Hope suggested. "He and Jolie are building a place a few minutes outside of town. I watch their little boy on—"

"Good evening, Hope. Tristan. I'd heard you were back. For the wedding, I presume?"

Hope looked desperately at the sidewalk underneath her feet, wishing it would open up and swallow her. But it stayed dismayingly solid. She wrapped her hands once more around her purse strap and turned around to face Bennett Ludlow, the head of the school board. The man had left his parked car and stood on the sidewalk behind them.

"Yes," Tristan said abruptly, barely sparing the other man a glance. "I'll drive you home, Hope."

His hand touched the small of her back, igniting a warm, melting glow.

"You mean you two were here together?" Bennett's white teeth smiled, but Hope knew the older man too well not to see the wheels clicking inside his brain. He was undoubtedly wondering the same thing Hope was. Why?

"Not really," Hope answered quickly. "And I think I'll walk home. It's such a lovely evening." She didn't dare look up into Tristan's face again. Every time she looked into his eyes, her sensible brain simply ground to a halt. And the last thing she needed was to look as muddled as she felt with Bennett there to witness it.

She wondered if she'd ever be able to forget that she'd been hired last year as a last resort because no other more qualified teacher had been available.

She smiled vaguely at both men and hurried across the street.

"She's not your usual type, is she, old boy?"

Irritation bubbled beneath Tristan's calm as he watched Hope reach the sidewalk on the other side of the street. He looked at Bennett. The attorney was as much a part of Weaver and the surrounding community as the Clays. More so than Tris, in fact. Because Bennett had returned to Weaver after college and Tris had not. Not that they'd ever had a lot to do with each other since Bennett was more Sawyer's age than Tristan's. "Should I be flattered you think you know my 'type,' Bennett?" he asked lazily. "Didn't think you cared."

Bennett's face tightened. "Before they moved away from Weaver, Gerri and Justine Leoni always were after a nice meal ticket, but I'd hoped that Hope had more sense than her mother and—"

"Go on inside and enjoy a steak," Tris smoothly interrupted. "Double-C beef, you know," he added as he started after Hope. "Can't be beat."

Certainly not by the failing spread that Bennett's parents had once run, long ago. They'd sold out to the Double-C more than twenty years earlier. As far as Tris knew, Bennett had hated the Clays ever since. And though Tris didn't give two hoots and a holler what Bennett thought or said about them, having that cap-toothed blowhard look down his nose at the Leonis—Hope in particular—was more than Tris could stand.

Hope. She was running away from him like the dogs of hell were at her heels. He wasn't so conceited that he believed all women found him irresistible. But he was wholly aware that Hope felt the same drugging attraction that he did, whether she admitted it or not.

He wanted her. Badly.

Seducing virgins was the one thing over which Tris drew the line. But a kiss was not a seduction.

He wanted to kiss her, and he knew she wanted it, too. But what had him going after her now was not the irrefutable urge to taste her lips, but the hurt in her eyes she hadn't been able to hide.

He quickened his step and caught up with her just as she was turning the corner toward her house. The hem of her white and purple flowered dress flared out behind her.

"Hold up there, sweet pea."

She looked over her shoulder once, but kept walking.

He swore silently and lengthened his stride, stepping in her path. She sidestepped, but he wasn't dancing. He closed his hands over her shoulder and she stopped cold. His gut tightened even more at the silvery trail wending its way down her sculpted cheekbones. "I'm sorry."

Her chin angled. "Don't flatter yourself."

He thumbed away a tear drop. "What are they for?"

"My shoes are pinching my feet," she said flatly. Red color flooded her cheeks.

Little liar. He hoped she never played poker. That milky pale skin of hers would give her away every time. He looked down at the confection of narrow straps and tiny heels gracing her feet. They were shamelessly feminine, sexy shoes and not at all what he'd expect her to wear with that ill-fitting sack of a dress. He crouched down, circling her ankle with his palm.

"What are you doing?" She pressed her palm to his shoulder, but he still managed to lift her foot and slide off the supposedly offending shoe. That was the nice thing about the element of surprise. He confiscated the other shoe, too, then swept her up into his arms.

She gasped, her eyes as wide as a child's. "What are you doing?"

"It's my fault your feet are hurting," he explained reasonably, looking down into her shocked face. "I said I'd give you a lift."

"A ride," she sputtered faintly.

He shrugged and turned up her street. He didn't dare think about how comfortable she felt in his arms, even squirming and kicking her legs the way she was. "What's the difference?"

"Well, one is in a car," she hissed. "Put me down before someone sees us—oh, fabulous."

"Hope? Is everything all right here?"

Hope smiled back at the openly curious question issued from a very pregnant woman who was watering a row of flowers in her yard. Tris noticed, however, that Hope's smile was frantic around the edges. "How are you feeling, Brenda? Your baby should be here any day now, right?"

"Next week," the other woman said. Her eyes were suspicious. "You sure you're okay?"

"She's fine," Tris said easily. "Stepped on a stone." He kept right on walking.

Even though he held Hope squarely in his arms, he could feel her straining as if to reduce the contact between their bodies. "Brenda Wyatt is one of the biggest gossips in the county," she muttered. "She's probably already heading to her phone to spread the word."

Tris cut across the corner of Hope's green lawn and carried her up the steps. A glance over his shoulder told him that Hope was probably right. Brenda-the-Blab was gone, and the screen door at the front of her house was swinging in the faint breeze because it hadn't caught the latch. "People in this town have always gossiped."

"Yes," Hope agreed tightly. "And half the time it's been about one of the infamous Leoni women, whether it was my mother or my sister." She leaned over and pushed open her front door. "Put me down."

Tris turned sideways and carried her into her living room. The furnishings were as uncomplicated as he'd expected: long lines and soft pillows, all in soft colors that reminded him of deliciously cool ice cream cones. "The only gossip I ever heard about your mother or your sister was that they were beautiful." He settled her on the couch where an enormous orange cat slept in a ball. "There. You're down."

"They were beautiful. Justine *is* beautiful. She's the kind of woman you should take out for steak."

"How is Justine, anyway? I haven't seen her in years." What he remembered about Justine was that she'd been, well, *popular* was the polite term. Before Justine and her mother had left town, she'd been ahead of him in school several years, but that hadn't meant that Tris hadn't appreciated her sultry appeal.

"She's in Washington State, now."

"Married?"

"Three times. And the people of this town thought she'd never find a husband with her wild, wicked ways," Hope quipped, but the sarcastic tone failed and she just sounded defensive. "Of course, she's divorcing number three, so maybe they had a point."

Tris sat on the couch, too, and Hope popped up like a golden-crisp slice of bread flying out of a toaster. He stretch his legs comfortably. "What does she do there?"

"She works in a bank. We don't talk much. She's older than you are." Hope had walked across the floor to look through the sheer, butter-yellow curtains that covered the big picture window overlooking her front yard. "Oh, nuts." She abruptly turned away from the window, drawing her eyebrows together.

"What's wrong?"

She shook her head and turned on the floor lamp that stood near the window. Bright light flooded the room, banishing the lengthening shadows. "Gram is driving up."

"Ruby? I haven't seen her in ages."

Hope glared at his left ear. "You don't understand at all, do you?"

Whatever was turning Hope's eyes to panic, he couldn't guess. But he understood all too well that the light was shining from behind Hope, turning her white sack dress with the tiny purple flowers into a *translucent* sack, barely veiling the long legs and hourglass curves beneath.

He ordered his heart to start beating again and inhaled slowly.

Hope's wiry grandmother walked right into the house without knocking. Her sharp eyes focused on Tris, then turned to Hope. But that one look left him feeling like he was fifteen again and had been caught making out with Suzette Lipton in the alley behind Ruby's Café. He was relieved he was sitting on the couch with the distance of the entire living room between him and Hope.

"I've had five calls at the café, young lady," Ruby said briskly, "all wanting to impart the news that my granddaughter was seen dancing down the middle of the streets with *him*. Now, I want to know what is going on!"

Tris laughed abruptly, which earned him another stern look from Ruby. He waited for Hope to explain, to defend herself, to tell her grandmother she was a grown woman who could do what she wanted if she chose, but Hope said nothing. She just stood there, looking at her grandmother with dismay emanating from every pore.

He rose and joined Hope, automatically sliding an arm around her shoulders, instinctively trying to support her. To alleviate the expression of dread darkening her eyes. "I carried her from the corner to this house," he said evenly. "Her feet were hurting her." He'd never felt strongly about explaining himself, and he didn't, even now. But he really hated the look on Hope's face. Really, really hated it.

It wasn't a comfortable realization. Because Tris never hated anything. He never hated and he never loved. He never felt that strongly one way or the other about anything. Except, maybe, his work. He was certainly a believer of the passion of the body, but he left all that passion of the heart to others.

Ruby's lips tightened. She propped her aging hands on her hips and ignored Tris. "Hope, you know how people in this town talk. Why would you do such a thing—right out in the street like that?"

"Ruby," Tris interrupted. He knew good and well that Hope's feet had been just fine. "Forget about it. There's no harm done."

Hope shook her head and turned away from her grandmother, pulling away from the arm that Tristan had tucked disturbingly around her shoulder.

"Young man," Ruby said sternly, "have you been gone from this town for so long you've forgotten how it operates? The only thing my granddaughter has is her reputation, and you come blowing into town for a few minutes of entertainment and destroy it without blinking."

"Gram!" Hope fastened her hands around her grandmother's arm and tugged her gently to the door. "Tristan was only being...kind," she said. "But he's going home, now. So you can go back to the café and tell everyone that nothing is going on."

"Hope, you're so innocent, girl. You wouldn't know a wolf in sheep's clothing if he bit you on the nose."

"Gram!" She couldn't bring herself to look at Tristan. She pulled her grandmother out the front door. "You are embarrassing me," she whispered under her breath.

"Everyone knows he lives in the fast lane—has ever since he earned all that money making fancy computer things," her grandmother said sternly. "If you're not careful he could take advantage of you just the way Justine and Gerri were."

"Tristan Clay's not the least bit interested in me that way."

"Ha!" Ruby headed down the path. "Open your eyes, girl. That man has got one thing on his mind, and sore feet is *not* it!"

Hope groaned and turned toward the door. She chewed the inside of her lip and prayed fervently that Tristan hadn't been able to hear her grandmother's outlandish worries.

She reached for the screen door and pulled it open, catching her breath when Tristan stepped right in front of her. Her fingers clenched over the door handle.

"Your grandmother is right." His face was hard, his jaw tight. And there was no trace of amusement in his heavy-lidded blue gaze. None at all. "I'm not interested in sore feet."

"Tristan, please. My grandmother is being ridiculous, I know that. I know you don't feel that way about—"

"I didn't say I didn't want to have you in my bed, Hope. I do. But no matter how much I want that, sweet pea, I don't intend to…deflower you. You're safe from me."

Chapter Four

*N*othing was going right today.

Hope's blow dryer blew a gasket or something, which meant that her hair was wet when she twisted it into a knot at the back of her head. She knew it looked even more unappealing than usual.

Of course, if she'd stuck to her guns the evening before and refused to join Tristan for dinner, Hope's hair would have been dry by the time she needed to leave for Sunday worship.

Even afterward, if she hadn't spent half the night swinging on a pendulum, she would have tended to business. But no, she'd paced around her small house, feeling astonishment. She'd rearranged her living room furniture twice, feeling disbelief. She'd yanked weeds under the moonlight in her backyard, feeling a fearful excitement.

So, her house was spotless, her furniture ended up right where it had been when she'd started and her garden was immaculate. But her hair was still a mess until morning.

Now, it was a wet, albeit clean, mess.

After the blow dryer had died, her iron—apparently sympathetic to the dryer—had shorted out, too. Her cotton dress was still presentable. Barely. Having to chase after Simon, her cat, at the last minute hadn't helped the dress. She'd been hot and frustrated by the time she finally coaxed him out from the bushes where he liked to hide.

At least she'd caught him before he'd prowled down to Brenda Wyatt's house. Brenda's husband hated cats, and Hope wasn't sure if her runaway cat would escape unscathed the next time he was caught eating Brenda's nasturtiums.

She could have driven her little car to church, but she knew there would be no parking left. And now, by the time she'd cut through the neighborhood and walked up the front steps of the church, she could hear the congregation inside already singing and she quietly slipped into the empty pew in the rear, fumbling a hymnal out of the rack. She dropped it and it thudded loudly on the floor just as the music ended.

It seemed as if half the town turned to look and see who'd made the racket. She smiled weakly and sat, feeling around with her hand for the hymnal, but it seemed to have scooted up under the pew ahead of her.

She still felt eyes watching her, and she wished

that she'd just taken the hint when the dryer died and stayed home.

Except if she hadn't shown up at church the way she had done every Sunday of every month of every year she'd lived in Weaver, she'd have ten people trooping by her house later to find out why.

After she'd come down with the flu last year when Ruby was in Washington visiting Justine, Hope's visitors had brought homemade soup and fresh flowers and crossword puzzles. She didn't think having visitors this time would be such a blessing.

The hairs on her neck prickled.

She blinked and saw Jolie staring at her pointedly from her seat on the aisle a few pews ahead. Hope frowned, shaking her head slightly.

Jolie rolled her eyes and subtly jabbed her thumb out. Hope followed the direction and stared, stunned at the sight of Tristan sitting there in church. There was no mistaking the back of his head; she'd never known anyone with hair that brilliantly golden.

She hurriedly closed her mouth and glanced at Jolie. Her friend was smiling, knowingly. Hope frowned at her, hoping Jolie could read her expression that there was no earthly reason to connect Hope with Tristan's once-in-a-blue-moon appearance at worship.

Feet shuffled and Hope dragged her attention to the service, as she stood with the rest of the congregation and read the gospel lesson. But her mind wasn't on the words. It was on the man three rows ahead of her.

When the service was winding down nearly an

hour later, Hope's attention still remained on Tristan. He hadn't turned around once to see her, and she told herself that she was relieved.

But she *was* sitting in church, and the lie tore at her. When the congregation rose once again to sing the last hymn, Hope quietly backed out of the church. If she ended up with calls from Gram and others that afternoon, it would be better than standing there visiting after the service, pretending that she didn't care two hoots that Tristan was around.

She pressed her hand to her forehead. She was a blooming fool, that's what she was. Creating ridiculous fantasies in her head.

Standing just outside the church doors, Tris watched Hope scurry away. It was definitely becoming too familiar a sight, he decided. He stopped and greeted the minister briefly, complimenting the man on his sermon even though he would've been pressed to recall the topic. He'd been too preoccupied with the young woman who'd sneaked in late to sit a few rows behind him.

"Guess no good deed goes unpunished," Sawyer said softly, mockingly, behind him.

Tris slid his sunglasses on and ignored his brother. So what if he'd come to church only in the hopes of catching Hope for a minute or two? What was more above-board than running into each other at church?

"Tristan, you're welcome to join us for dinner this afternoon," said Rebecca, repeating the invitation that he'd already declined once. "I know Ryan wants to have a chance to talk your ear off about his new computer.''

Tris tugged on the bill of Ryan's ball cap. ''Maybe later. But don't hold up the meal if I don't show.''

Ryan grinned and darted off to join his friend. Sawyer slid his arm around Rebecca's shoulders and snorted softly. ''Tris, if your rental car is seen in town anywhere this afternoon other than at our place, the remaining half of this town that hasn't been talking about your *stroll* down the street with Hope yesterday, will be. Leave her alone.''

''Sawyer, don't pick on Tristan like that.''

''He's a big boy, Bec, and you don't know what he's like with women.''

Tristan's good humor was fading fast. ''And you're so sure *you* know?'' he asked Sawyer. ''I thought you were a big believer in the innocent-'til-proven theory.''

''You haven't been innocent since you were fifteen,'' Sawyer replied dryly. ''You're gonna do what you're gonna do no matter what anyone says. Just…remember where you are.''

Rebecca was making a face. ''Sawyer's a fine one to talk.'' She stretched up and kissed Tristan's cheek. ''Maybe we'll see you later,'' she said calmly, then looked at her husband. ''Ryan is going home with Eric for a while,'' she said softly.

Despite his annoyance, Tris felt a smile tug at him as Sawyer cast his wife a long look, then smiled slowly as they walked away. He pulled the car keys out of his pocket and started toward the small, still-congested lot. Most of the cars belonged to people who'd driven in from the outlying areas, since the town itself was small enough to walk pretty well anywhere.

But, as he approached his car, he realized that a van parked crookedly in the lot was responsible for the holdup. He shook his head faintly and cut between two pickups. He wanted to go by Hope's place. Maybe he could talk her into going for a drive. They could invite Drew and his wife if it would put Hope more at ease. He knew she and Jolie were friends—

"Mr. Clay, is it true that you and Ms. Leoni are living together?"

He jerked around, gravel grinding under his boot and came face-to-face with a microphone and an enormous camera. "What the hell?" The microphone shoved closer and he pushed it away. "Get out of my face."

"You've been out of the public eye for nearly seven years now." The strident female voice wasn't discouraged. "You were on the road to success the likes of which we've only seen in Bill Gates. Has the pressure been too much for you? Are you moving back to this quaint little town where you came from? Do you still speak with Serena Stevenson? She moved recently to San Diego, and it's known that you own property there. Does she know of Ms. Leoni's pregnancy?"

Tris grabbed the hand that held the microphone and pulled, yanking the hair-sprayed, brittle reporter close enough to see the flicker of unease in her calculating eyes. But he suddenly became aware of the hush around them, of the intrusive camera not two feet away from him. He clenched his jaw and slowly released the reporter's wrist. He stared hard at her. The reporter was on a fishing expedition pure and simple, and he'd already given her more reaction than she deserved. "No comment."

Every fiber in him wanted to shove the words back down the reporter's throat, but he knew better. So he turned away and yanked open the car door, sliding behind the wheel. It had been many years since he'd had to deal with the media, but he hadn't forgotten the lessons he'd learned.

Serena had been an expert at drawing the press's attention, but then, as a high-priced fashion model, she'd wanted it.

He barely kept himself from gunning the engine. The van—he realized now it belonged to the news crew—was still blocking the driveway and he turned the wheels sharply and drove over the grass, jouncing over the curb and out onto the side street.

In his rearview mirror, he could see the cameraman jogging toward the van. He swore softly. There was no way he could go by Hope's place now. They'd likely follow him.

"Pregnant," he muttered, shaking his head. He'd have to make a few calls and find out who on earth had instigated the story. It would've had to be someone right here in Weaver spinning tales. It must be the slowest news day in history for a crew to drive down from Gillette on such a sorry excuse. His profile these days was so low it was nonexistent.

Turning the car out of town, Tris grimaced. There were some days when nothing went right.

Unfortunately, back at the big house, he had no

doubt that wedding fever continued reigning supreme. If he went back now, he'd be expected to tie bows for his sisters-in-law, or trim back the lilac bushes or, God forbid, help Matt and Dan with the chores.

Didn't seem to matter that the Double-C had year-round hands now, and had done for some time. When a Clay boy put his foot on Double-C land, he was expected to carry his weight. Tris held that belief, too. He was just sick to death of the wedding noise.

It was one thing for the women to talk about it. That was a female kind of thing. But it was another thing for his brothers to jabber about it, too. And if it wasn't Matthew, Daniel and Jefferson as well if he was around, gnawing on the chew toy of happiness that their women had brought into their lives, then it was the old man himself wanting to know when Tris was "gonna grow up and stop playing with his damned computers."

Which meant, in Squire-speak, "When are you gonna move back home where you belong?"

Tris was glad his cantankerous father was finally getting married to his sweetheart. Gloria Day was a great lady. She'd stood up to Squire right from the beginning, when she'd been his nurse after his heart attack. She had grit, and Tris admired grit.

He still wished that Gloria and Squire had eloped or something, rather than wait until summertime when Gloria's daughters were finally out of college.

If they had, Tris wouldn't be here in Wyoming now, and some damned fool reporter with nothing better to do wouldn't be speculating on his relation-

ship with *Ms. Leoni.* He wouldn't have run into
Hope at all, for that matter.

Swearing under his breath, Tris pulled a U-turn
right in the middle of the highway and drove back
toward Weaver. He didn't let his family dictate his
actions and he'd be damned if he'd let some idiot
reporter do it, either.

He drove past the now-empty church parking lot
and tracked down Jolie and Drew at the pizza parlor,
where Evan was tumbling around in a big cage with
a bunch of colorful baseball-sized plastic balls. Jolie
grinned like a fiend when he joined them, and she
quickly scurried off to the phone when he casually
mentioned Hope's name.

Colbys had been a bust, and church hadn't been
much better. Maybe the third time would be the
charm.

The restaurant was packed with the after-church
crowd. Ryan and his friend were there and Tris—
glad of a reason not to be caught watching the door
in case Hope *did* show—joined the two boys at the
video-game machines.

One of the games was new, he noticed with
amusement. There was even a line of kids waiting
to play it. He left Ryan and Eric and stood off to
the side, watching the player—a girl of about nine
or ten, probably—stare fiercely at the screen, one
hand clenched around the joystick, one hand hovering over the button controls.

She needed to relax the joystick, Tris thought absently. She wouldn't make it to the third level if her
reactions were slowed by that too-tight grip. And the
third level was where he'd programmed the dragon

to appear, set on stealing away the princess who guarded all of the magical secrets that the player needed to uncover.

Tris slowly turned his head, looking toward the doorway. Hope stood there, and from his vantage point, he could see her eyes drifting over the crowded tables until she found Jolie and Drew. She still wore the pale pink cotton dress she'd worn to church, and with her hair screwed back into that mind-numbingly tight bun, Tris couldn't decide if she was trying to look fourteen or forty.

It didn't matter. He'd known women who seemingly wouldn't draw a second glance from a gnat and women whom the world considered its most beautiful. The surface was only so much trappings, and the woman inside held the wealth of her nature—good or bad. Sometimes both.

Underneath Hope's girl-woman exterior lay what? Innocence? Certainly. Passion? Very probably.

He headed toward her, watching her head lift like a wary animal sensing danger. Her fingertips crept to the necklace that she seemed to wear as a talisman.

He caught the pained look she directed at Jolie, but he kept walking toward Hope. She looked from side to side, then firmed her shoulders and looked him straight on—in the chin.

"I'm not the wolf set to gobble down the girl," he murmured. "So I hope you won't run away from me again like you did this morning."

"I wasn't—oh, I knew I should have gone with Gram instead of coming here."

"Where's Gram?"

"Gone to a quilting show."

"Do you quilt?"

"No, but—"

"Then why go?"

"Because...because the quilts are beautiful."

"I don't doubt it. Several quilts at the ranch were made by my mother. Doesn't mean I want to go looking at a room full of 'em."

"*You* weren't invited," she said, "so I guess you don't have to worry about that."

He smiled faintly. "What worries *you?* What I told you yesterday?"

Her cheeks filled with color. "You shouldn't talk that way. Someone might overhear."

Which reminded him soundly of the reporter and cameraman. "And start to speculate on when the baby is due?"

Her eyes widened. So he told her briefly about the incident. "I wouldn't worry about it much if I were you. There's no story for them here. Nothing will come of it."

"But they asked you right out if I was...um, uh—"

"Pregnant," he supplied. "And it wasn't exactly a question. They just wanted a reaction from me on tape."

"And there were still people in the parking lot who overheard it?"

He shrugged. "The van blocked the drive so nobody could get out. I don't think you need to worry about it, sweet pea, but it is remotely possible that you might get a call for an interview or something."

"Because I'm supposed to be having your baby," she said flatly. "Well, Gram is going to love that."

He touched her shoulder, wishing she'd relax. "It's all bull, Hope. Ignore it. Or, if the reporter does happen to call, give her an earful if it makes you feel better. I'm telling you, though, they'll lose interest, if they haven't already, the second a hotter story comes along."

"Why were you—" She frowned and looked around her, lowering her voice again. "Why were you at church in the first place?"

"Why do you think?"

Her eyes glanced up at him and away. "Seeking forgiveness?"

"Seeking you."

Her throat worked. "You didn't even know I was there."

He nudged her out the entrance they were blocking, and along the sidewalk a few feet. "You arrived exactly twelve-and-a-half minutes into the service, sat in the corner of the back row and left during the first verse of the last song."

"Hymn."

"Whatever. Do your shoes pinch your feet today?"

"What?"

"Let's walk. We'll stay right here on Main, in full view of anyone who cares to look."

"But I thought you were here for pizza with the Taggarts."

"I wouldn't want to impose on them. Walk with me, Hope."

She drew her eyebrows together. "I *do not* understand you. At all."

"If we stand here for one second more," he leaned closer so only she could hear, "I'm going to kiss you regardless of who is watching through the window." He watched her slender throat work. And decided that he wasn't sure he wouldn't *anyway*. "It won't matter that there is no reporter around to spread the word—the gossip-mill of Weaver will do the job quite well on its own."

He could see the indecision in her eyes. "If I promise to keep my hands to myself?" he added blandly.

She huffed and started walking briskly down the sidewalk. Tris hid a smile and easily caught up with her.

They walked for several minutes, passing people now and again. Some familiar to him. Some not. But they all greeted Hope and eyed him closely.

Almost as closely as Hope did when she looked sideways at him. "Are you bored or something?"

Amusement lightened his mood. "Not at all. Surprising, actually, because I've never been all that big a fan of small town life."

"You never had small-town life," she pointed out. "You lived well outside of Weaver on an extremely busy ranch."

"Close enough. Went to school here in town."

She shook her head. "That's not what I meant, anyway."

She was walking so fast, they'd already come to the corner that turned onto her street. He caught her hand and crossed diagonally to the park. The play equipment was deserted, and he tugged her along with him to the swings. He grabbed one and jiggled it invitingly. "Then what?"

She stared at the swing. Then at him. "You want to *swing?*"

"You do."

"No, I don't."

He shook the swing again, making the curving seat bounce and the chains clank. "When was the last time you rode a swing? Come on. You know you want to. I saw you playing with my nieces yesterday, remember? Any self-respecting kindergarten-through-third grade teacher who can blow the mean bubbles you did *definitely* wants to swing in the park on a sunny Sunday afternoon."

The smile on her face was unwilling, but it was there. "You're a nut."

"So I've been told. Come on. Up and at 'em."

She turned and, gathering her dress around her legs, sat on the swing. He heard her suck in her breath when he pulled the swing way back and let it fly. Again and again he pushed, watching her legs stretch out before her as she soared way, way, up. Then down and back and down and up.

Her laughter floated on the breeze. "I think you're bored, and flirting with someone like me is just a way of passing the time for you," she called down to him.

He stepped to the side of her swing. She didn't need him behind, pushing. She was flying all on her own. "What do you mean, someone like you?"

Down and back. He saw her roll her eyes. "You know what I mean."

He caught the chains, dragging the swing to a shuddering halt and wrapped his arms around her waist. Only because of her startled grip around the chains did she remain in the seat of the swing. Her bare calves were all but straddling his thighs. "So you want to pretend that there is no attraction between us."

Her lips parted. "I—"

"And pretend that you weren't trembling yesterday in my arms." He drew her an inch closer.

"Don't. Somebody might see."

"What? Two people in broad daylight in the park?" A few more inches closer and she was as high as his waist. It took all of his willpower not to close his hands around her thighs and pull them right around him. And maybe that was why the fire in his gut burned so unbearably bright. The fact that he wouldn't.

Because she was right. Someone might see them. And though they were respectably public, the urge to pull her softness against him—to let her know just exactly what he felt for "someone like her"— was intimately private.

He forced a smile and pushed her and the swing back so far that he could step under it. He let go and she went shooting up into the sky and the moment passed.

Leaving them just a guy and a pink-dressed woman and a swing. Which was fine with him, Tris reminded himself. Exactly the way it should be. The only thing it could be for a man who was as incapable of love as the computers he designed.

Chapter Five

Tris propped his elbows on the gleaming surface of the bar in Colbys and looked around. The bar was packed. Seemed as if half the state of Wyoming had turned out for Squire's bachelor party.

He stifled a sigh and lifted the glass, throwing back half the drink with a grimace. He started for the pool table where Daniel had been reigning, and absently pulled a cue from the rack on the wall.

Jefferson looked over his shoulder at him when he stopped behind him. "Dan's cleaned up," he said.

Tris smiled faintly. "He usually does." Dan was whistling tunelessly, pocketing the money he'd won from the other players before racking the balls again.

By the time he was finished, Sawyer and Matthew had joined them. Matthew broke, and the game was on. And still, Tris felt about as celebratory as a turtle. When it was his shot, he leaned over the table and missed a shot he should have made in his sleep.

"You're not still hung up on the mess Beaudreau made of the Pirelli deal, are you?" Jefferson spoke quietly.

Tris shoved the pool cue back in the rack on the wall. The truth was, he hadn't thought about the case awaiting him in Paris in days. And having his older brother bring up the sticky situation just proved that Jefferson wasn't as out of the loop of Hollins-Winword as he'd have everyone believe. "We got it under control before I left."

"Then you're still thinking about Hope Leoni."

He turned his back on Jefferson, ignoring his observation. But his brother, the one he'd probably been closest to, didn't let it go so easily and followed Tris over to the bar. "Give it a rest, would you?" He glared at his brother and picked up his drink. "I swear, I'd rather hear you wax poetic about marriage and kids."

Jefferson wasn't deterred, even though he smiled faintly at the poetic thing. Nobody had ever accused Jefferson of being talkative. "She's a sweet kid. The story of you pushing her on the swing in the park has made the news wire."

"Not quite," Tris countered. It was an exaggeration, but only slightly. "And I haven't seen Hope since Tuesday, so just drop it."

He'd finally managed to have a meal with Hope— at Drew and Jolie's place while she babysat for young Evan. He'd shown up with cartons of Chinese that he'd had to drive fifty miles to get. She'd looked at him like he was crazy, but she'd let him in. She'd heated the food in the microwave, and the two of them had played video games with Evan until the little boy was ready to fall asleep with the controls in his hand. Drew and Jolie had arrived soon after, and Tris had driven out to the ranch. Pure and simple.

"This big, bad wolf is staying well away from the town virgin." Even if he had been driven from his own bed in the middle of the night after that "pure and simple" evening because he couldn't get the woman out of his head.

Jefferson leaned his elbows on the bar. "It's hard to have the hots for an innocent young woman," he murmured. "No pun intended."

"What is hard," Tris said between his teeth, "is having everyone in this damned town thinking they know some dirty secret about Hope and me. *Nothing* has happened between us." If you didn't count the thoughts he'd had, that was. "Christ, Jefferson, even you warned me to behave around her. Like I couldn't figure that out for myself."

"Well, kid, you haven't exactly been known for your restraint. Em says you had women coming and going when she lived at your place. Must've been your pretty face."

"Em talks too much," Tris muttered, lifting his drink. If he hadn't earned a bloody fortune designing computer programs when he'd been younger than Hope, he would never have been in the position of having women throwing themselves at him at every turn. All he'd wanted back then was to do his own thing, coming up with stronger, more-powerful, less-expensive software. His fledgling company had taken off like a bullet, bringing him money and women. Then more money and more women. Then, on a whim as much as anything—mostly because he'd needed something challenging to keep his mind off the callous way he'd hurt one woman in particular—he'd hacked into one-too-many systems and found himself in a whole other kettle of fish.

He couldn't believe after all these years that his name was once again being stuck in an ongoing news story—that of the former tycoon who was corrupting the schoolmarm. The reporter had even gotten hold of Tristan's old school records, as if the randy behavior of the adolescent was being relived by the grown man.

"You should've known better than to try to meet her at church," Jefferson murmured.

Tris turned and gestured at Newt for another whiskey. "I went to church because I wanted to hear a good sermon."

Jefferson snorted. "Blatant lies don't get you into heaven, kid. You even chased her around town, ending up in the park."

"We weren't doing anything wrong." The film crew had caught only a hazy shot of Tris pushing Hope on the swing. "I can't help it if that crazy reporter is pushing us as the next great… Hell, I don't even know what they're pushing."

"They're speculating on whether the good girl can tame the bad boy, or whether the bad boy is ruining the good girl. Same thing everyone in town is wondering."

"It's none of their damned business," Tris said

irritably. The reporter hadn't stopped after the park swing incident, and had caught Hope just yesterday. "If Hope had only locked herself in at the café instead of trying to beat them home, the only thing the cameraman would have been able to film would have been the exterior of the café." Instead, footage of Hope—head bowed against the questions being pelted at her by the reporter as she ran away down the street in her pink waitress uniform—had been seen in one form or another on everything from the local news to a syndicated gossip show.

"You're accustomed to dealing with the press— at least you used to be. Hope isn't. Where is she, anyway?"

Tris looked down at his drink. "Home, I think." He knew she wasn't at Ruby's because Jolie had told him so when he'd called to talk to Drew.

Thanks to posting some key hands at the gates of the Double-C, the reporter and her crew hadn't been able to get near the ranch. And Colbys was locked up tighter than a drum tonight against any unknown faces. But Hope? What the hell had he done to protect Hope?

Not one damned thing.

Tris hated it all. He hated feeling so strongly about anything, and he hated the fact that he hadn't been able to help Hope in the slightest. Or perhaps it was just his conscience nagging him because he'd brought all this down on her head. Because he had the "hots," to use his brother's ironic word.

Jefferson ought to know, since he'd had it bad for Emily for years before he'd ever made a move. Because Em was younger. Innocent.

There was a severe difference, though, Tris knew. He tossed back another shot of whiskey and absently noticed that the lights around the room were starting to blur. Thank goodness the women were at their own party—a nonalcoholic one—and would pick up the men to go home later.

He frowned. Difference. Right. The difference between Jefferson and Tris was the fact that Jefferson had loved Emily all along. Tris, though, didn't love any woman. He might enjoy sleeping with them, and he was damn sure he'd really enjoy spreading Hope's toffee-colored hair over a pillowcase and tracing the trail of her necklace down to her breasts. But that was sex. Not love. He didn't love her. He couldn't love her.

It wasn't in him to love anyone. He'd designed impenetrable computer systems; as impenetrable as one could be anyway. He knew computers inside and out. Hell, he had a computer chip for a heart. Isn't that what Serena had accused him of years ago?

She'd been right.

Tris had teased Hope, flirted with her because he liked seeing that rosy blush rise in her cheeks, and he'd wanted to taste her lips. Now she had Wyoming's own version of paparazzi hounding her.

He had to see her, he thought fuzzily. He had to fix it. He looked over at Jefferson—blinked when he realized his brother wasn't even sitting on the bar stool anymore, but had returned to the pool game. Tris focused on the exit he could see through the kitchen and headed for it.

* * *

Hope checked both doors to make sure they were locked, then all the windows to be certain the shades and curtains were drawn, before she let herself relax enough to take a quick shower. She'd never felt so unnerved in her life. In less than a week, her life had become a circus sideshow. All because of Tristan Clay.

If only she could make herself be angry with him. Lastingly angry, that was. The kind that would stick. Rather than the kind that dissipated the moment she looked at his ridiculously handsome face. It didn't even have to be in person. All she had to do was see his image on the television screen in some old story the media had dug up from years ago and her anger drained away. She was left feeling lightheaded and limp and remembering the moments on the swing in the park; remembering the statement he'd made even before that.

Tristan Clay wanted boring Hope Leoni.

It boggled the mind. It agitated her tummy. It left her warm and aching and altogether edgy and even a soothing shower failed to alleviate any of it.

She was just combing out her wet hair when she heard the thump at the rear of her house. Her heart raced. If it was that reporter, she was going to call the sheriff whether he was still at his father's bachelor party, or not. She set down her comb and turned the light off in her bedroom, then crept down the hallway.

Another thump made her gasp aloud.

She sidled into the kitchen. The back door was locked. She'd checked it twice. But as she watched, the knob started turning. The door creaked, the door opened, she heard a soft oath and a large, dark shape loomed in the doorway.

Hope screeched and reacted. She grabbed the cordless phone off the wall and launched it directly at the body and darted down the hall toward the front door, intent only on getting out of the house as rapidly as possible.

She only made it as far as the couch in the living room when an iron arm clamped around her waist, halting her flight. She kicked out, but her feet were bare. She'd have kneed him—for it was a *he* she was certain—only he had her from behind. She used her elbow sharply, earning a muffled grunt. And then she lowered her head, sinking her teeth into the back of the pig's hand—

"Dammittohell, Hope!"

He let her loose and she tumbled over the arm of the couch, falling inelegantly to the floor. Then suddenly, the light was on and Tristan was staring at her from across the room, his hand on the floor lamp near the front window.

Hope adjusted her glasses and stared. "What on earth are you doing?" She pressed her hand to her heart, willing it to stop thundering.

"Getting my hand bit off," he growled. "Couldn't you hear me calling your name?"

She drew the folds of her cotton robe closer together and scrambled up from the floor onto the couch. Her heart still felt ready to explode right out of her chest. "All I heard was a few thumps, and then you were breaking into my kitchen." She drew in a hard breath. "Are you *insane?*"

"I didn't break in," he said, rather more clearly

than necessary. "I—well, mebbe I picked the lock," he admitted. "I came to rescue you." He smiled.

"Rescue me from what?"

"The pap-razzi." He frowned, looking around the living room.

"I *thought* you were that hideous reporter," Hope muttered. She pushed her hair out of her eyes and focused more clearly on him. He wore black jeans and an ivory shirt that flowed smoothly over his broad shoulders. "You shouldn't be here."

He nodded, utterly serious. Then abruptly sat on the arm of the cushioned chair beside the lamp. "I know. I'm a sorry SOB. It's all my fault." He squinted at her. "I knew your hair would reach your...ah...fanny if it wasn't braided. "

Hope flushed from the roots of her hair to that other part he'd just mentioned. She felt the heat just flood through her like a switch had been thrown on. "You're drunk."

He frowned. Sighed. "No. Not much." Then he smiled faintly. "I found the right house from the alley side."

She almost smiled, completely forgetting that she was going to tell him he had to leave. It was nearly midnight. "You...ah, didn't tell anyone you were coming here, did you?"

He shook his head, holding up his hand. "No more'n I told anyone about Tuesday at the Taggarts. Scout's honor."

She stood and tightened the sash on her ankle-length robe. She knew Jolie and Drew weren't likely to gossip about Tristan's unexpected visit while

Hope was watching Evan. "Were you ever a boy scout?"

He grinned wickedly. "Whatdya think?"

She groaned and turned toward the kitchen. She closed the back door that had been left open, hung up the phone that had miraculously remained intact and started a pot of strong coffee. When she turned around again, it was to find Tristan standing just a few feet behind her. She sucked in her breath, pressing her hand against her heart. "Stop sneaking around on me!"

"Sweet pea, I'd never sneak around on you," he said distinctly, giving the words an entirely different spin that made her cheeks heat all over again.

She frowned severely. "Have you eaten?"

He shrugged. "Sure."

"When?" She stepped past him toward the refrigerator, dragging her eyes from the waist of his jeans that looked as if they hung just a little too loosely from his hips. "Oh, for goodness sake, Tristan, you're swaying. Sit down before you fall on your face." She yanked open the door and pulled out the roast that she'd made in the Crock-Pot earlier that day.

His eyes followed the food. "Please don't be a good cook," he muttered.

He was half-drunk, she reminded herself. "Okay, I won't. But I can't be expected to drive miles to pick up Chinese if I'm not inclined to cook or order pizza here in town." She *was* Ruby Leoni's granddaughter, after all, and had grown up in her kitchen. She sliced off a thick wedge of beef and scooped vegetables on the plate, heated the whole lot in the microwave while the coffee finished perking, and set the meal in front of him at the table.

Without a word, he picked up the fork and dove in. But when she started to leave the kitchen, intent on donning something more suitable, more sensible, than her pale-green robe, he caught her wrist and tugged her back down to the seat beside him. "Stay with me."

Hope yanked her robe over her knees. "You shouldn't be here, Tristan," she said again.

He didn't disagree. Just popped a tender piece of carrot into his mouth. "I should've known you could cook," he said eventually, when his plate was scraped clean and the lingering bleariness had nearly been eradicated from his eyes. "You'll be a perfect wife for some lucky guy one day."

Hope swallowed and retrieved the coffee pot to refill his cup. His eyes met hers. She stopped pouring and set the pot on the table. "According to the six o'clock news yesterday, half the state apparently thinks I'm going to make *you* a perfect wife." She couldn't believe the bold words had come from her own lips. If the surprise in his sapphire eyes was any indication, he couldn't believe it, either.

"But I'd make the worst husband. I didn't mean to bring this all down on your head, Hope," he said quietly. "I just—hell, I just wanted to spend some time with a pretty woman."

Her fingers twisted the ends of her sash into knots. "I'm not pretty. I'm not…anything. That's why everybody is making such a fuss. Because you're so—" She couldn't finish that. Not without bringing fresh mortification upon herself. He was wealthy, spectacularly handsome and decidedly mysterious since he'd disappeared from the public eye. She was…none of those things.

"That reporter is Brenda Wyatt's cousin, you know," she said, instead. "That's how this insanity began. Brenda was probably on the phone the minute she realized it was Tristan Clay carrying the hometown nobody down the street."

"You need to look in a mirror more often, sweet pea, and get rid of this notion that you have no appeal." He stared into his coffee. "You can stay at the Double-C until the reporter-from-hell loses interest."

Hope swallowed.

"Nobody gets on the property who doesn't belong there," he continued.

"I still have to help Gram during the week," she countered, even though she knew Gram could get one of the high school kids to help her out. He'd made the offer only because he wanted to protect her. It was impossibly sweet. But even contemplating the notion shook her to the core. "I won't let that reporter person make me hide," she added.

He smiled faintly. "Grit. Good for you."

"And you'll be gone soon, anyway." She didn't like thinking about that just yet, but it was a fact. "They can hardly make a, uh, a romance—sleazy, or a fairy tale—out of anything when you're not even here. Right?"

"Brenda Wyatt's kid is gonna be born with two heads," he said, rather than answer.

"Don't be mean." She nibbled the inside of her

lip. "Destined to become a gossip columnist is far more likely."

He stared. Then barked with laughter.

Hope couldn't help but smile. But then his eyes touched on her lips and she swallowed, staring down at the edge of her robe that her fingers were nervously pleating.

He cleared his throat, then drained the rest of his coffee. "Thanks for the meal. I think I can walk a straight line, now."

Feeling awkward, Hope managed a smile. "You can probably slip back into the bachelor party with nobody the wiser." She wanted, desperately, to ask him why he hadn't just stayed at Colbys where she'd heard a veritable feast had been planned for the party-goers.

He didn't look very enthusiastic about the suggestion, however. "Mind if I finish the coffee first?"

"No, of course not." She snatched up the pot and reached over to pour it in his cup, but he moved the cup toward her at the same time, and the hot liquid hit the table, splashing the front of his shirt.

He stood abruptly, yanking his sodden shirt away from his abdomen. Hope set down the pot, pressing her hands to her cheeks in horror. "I'm so sorry," she gasped. "I c-can't believe I did that again." She dashed around and pulled at the top button. "Take it off so I can get the stain out before it ruins your shirt."

"Don't worry about it."

"Please, it's the least I can do."

He raked his fingers through his hair, disheveling

the thick gold mass. "Sweet pea, taking off my shirt isn't a real good idea."

"Don't be ridiculous. It shouldn't take long for me to rinse out the stain."

Tris ignored the lingering scorch of the coffee that had burned through the shirt against his stomach. The burn ignited by Hope's fluttering fingers tugging at the collar of his shirt was another matter. "Hope."

"What?"

One look into her violet eyes and he knew she was just one big bundle of nerves. Another weight clanged into place on his conscience. One of her hands crept nervously to her gold necklace. He deliberately lifted his gaze from the beguiling shadow in the vee of her robe lapels. It didn't even bear thinking about what she had on beneath the cotton. Or didn't.

He touched her necklace with his fingertip and she went abruptly, painfully, still. "You always wear this," he murmured. "Don't you?"

Her long throat worked. She nodded. "Since I was twelve years old and snooping in Gram's attic for her dresses from Italy when she was young. I, uh, I found it in a jewelry box."

When he hooked his finger beneath the fine gold links, he was even more aware of the satiny texture of her skin beneath. Warm and fragrant with the lilac scent of her. He slowly drew the chain upward, watching the pulse beat visibly in her throat, feeling his own drum heavily in response.

The chain was long. Long enough to lay nestled between her breasts, he realized with a silent groan.

And at the end of it hung a skin-warmed wedding band. Too large to be a woman's, he noticed. "And this? You found this, too?"

She caught her lip between her teeth. Then exhaled audibly and stepped back. Not too far back, however, because he still held the ring.

"Gram told me it was my mother's. That she'd been saving it for the love of her life."

The ring was plain, with no inscription, and was large enough to slide over his finger. "And now you're saving it for the love of your life?"

She lifted her shoulder, not answering. But he knew he'd guessed accurately. He let go of the ring and it settled against her robe. "Do you miss her?"

Hope turned away, busily mopping up the spilled coffee. "It's hard to miss what you never knew. She died when I was two. That's when Gram brought me back to Weaver to live with her. Justine was already out on her own by then."

His mother had died in childbirth with him. Only when it was late at night and he was trying not to think about a violet-eyed temptress would he admit that he missed his mother. Missed never having known her.

He still felt guilty deep down in his gut for even existing. Which was something he wouldn't think about no matter what the circumstances. "So Ruby stepped in, becoming the mother you'd lost," he concluded abruptly.

Hope nodded. "Will you let me clean that stain, now?"

Because it seemed so important to her, he flicked open the buttons and shrugged out of it, handing it to her. She avoided looking at him and disappeared into a little room off the kitchen. The laundry room, he assumed.

He took his plate and flatware to the sink and rinsed them, then wiped up the last bit of spill from the floor. Hope still hadn't emerged and he scrubbed his hands over his face.

He could go now, but appearing at the bachelor party without his shirt was probably not a good move.

Hell, he hadn't been making good moves since he'd arrived in Weaver last week. And he was supposed to be a fairly intelligent guy.

He tilted his head, hearing an odd scraping sound. His first thought was that someone had followed him. But then he dismissed it. Paranoia on his part wouldn't help anything.

Suddenly, Hope reappeared. "Did you hear that noise?"

"Yeah."

She huffed and darted past him, opening the kitchen door and looking out. "Simon? Simon are you out there?" Huffing again, she shut the door and stepped around him into the hall.

"Who the hell is Simon?" He followed.

"My cat." She dashed aside the curtains on her front window. "Darnitall, he got out through the window again."

"If that's a problem, maybe you should shut it," Tris murmured, standing to the side and looking over her head at the side-sliding window.

She frowned, sliding it the few inches until it was closed once more. "I do. He opens it."

"A cat who opens windows. Now *that* is interesting news for Brenda-the-Blab's cousin."

Hope turned, froze for a second when she found him standing right behind her, then moved over to the front door and yanked it open. "Yes, well, Simon seems to have a thing for the Wyatt's flowers, and I'd better find him before Brenda's husband does." She gathered the long folds of her robe around her and went out into the dark.

Tris closed his eyes, hoping like hell that Brenda's cousin wasn't camped out in some ridiculous vantage-point at the school or park across the street. He strode after Hope, catching up to her quickly. "I'll find the cat."

She was looking toward the Wyatt's house, where the flowers grew profusely against the fence. "I know the spot he goes to."

He physically turned her toward her own house. "I'll find the cat," he repeated. "You're wearing a robe."

Her lips parted. She looked down at herself, then nodded and hurried back toward the light shining out her front door. He could hear her muttering to herself as she went. "Stupid, stupid, stupid," she was saying.

Tris watched her until she entered her house. Then he blew out a long breath and crossed the lawn of the house next door to the Wyatts'. He crouched down, peering through the foliage and fence. "Simon," he grumbled. "Get your tail outta there before we all get caught."

The beast didn't appear. Naturally. But it did let out a howl loud enough to wake the dead. "I hate cats.'' Tris followed the sound of the meowing back between the two houses. He looked around, and seeing nobody—no shifting shadows that might indicate someone—stepped over the white pickets. His shoes squished in the slippery mud and he slid, grabbing onto the first thing he could. The leafy plants came right out of the ground in his fist just as his hip banged hard against the fence. He barely caught himself from landing butt-first in the mud. And still, nobody came running from either house to see who was making the racket.

Shoving the uprooted plant back into the mud, Tris gave the fence a good shake, relieved to find it held firm. All he needed was to have to own up to knocking down a fence in the middle of the night and he'd complete the picture of being a teenager, sneaking around in the middle of the night with his buddy, Drew, when they were supposed to be back at Drew's house, sleeping soundly. If any of Coleman Black's guys could see him now, nobody at Hollins-Winword would ever take him seriously again.

The moon was high and bright and Tris eventually found the cat huddling under a plant, chewing merrily away on a flower. He scooped up the feline, for which he earned a stinging scratch, hopped the fence and jogged back to Hope's house, holding the cat out at a safe distance.

Hope had left the front door open and he wiped his muddy shoes before going inside. He pushed the door shut and held out the cat to Hope. ''Put a lock on the window,'' he suggested dryly, watching her bury her nose in the cat's tabby-orange ruff.

"Thank you for finding him," she said gratefully. The cat jumped out of her arms, sidled around her bare feet, looked up at Tristan disdainfully, then hopped onto the couch where he turned a few circles and settled himself in the corner. "Simon thanks you, too."

"Oh yeah, I can tell," he said dryly. He wondered if the bachelor party was still going on. He'd been at Hope's more than an hour.

"You've scratched yourself," Hope murmured, her eyes distressed.

Tris looked over at the cat.

"Simon? Now I really feel awful. Let me get something to clean it up." She turned in a whirl of green cotton and damp hair and was back in seconds, a gauze pad in one hand and a bottle of rubbing alcohol in the other.

"It might sting a bit," she murmured and pressed the wet pad against his rib where the cat had left his "thank you."

Tris sucked in his breath. "A bit?" He laughed and winced all at once and caught her dabbing hand before she could torment and torture him even more. "It's fine, sweet pea. It's late and I should go. Why don't you give me my shirt and I'll—"

"Oh! Yes, yes, of course." She held the gauze and the alcohol close against her and scurried away again.

He must be out of his mind, he thought, shoving his hands through his hair as he followed. She came out of the kitchen, shirt in hand. Her eyes flitted nervously over his chest, then away.

He took the shirt from her and yanked the damp

fabric over his shoulders, not bothering to button it. The hall seemed too narrow, her lilac-scented body too close. In some portion of his mind, he knew he should get out of there. But when he reached out and threaded his fingertips through the damp hair at her temple and gently drew the dark locks away from her ivory face, he couldn't for the life of him think why.

"Tristan," she whispered, her gaze finally flying to his. "You have to go."

Knowing she was right didn't help his conscience any. Nor did it prevent him taking a step nearer to her. "No one knows I'm here, sweet pea, except your fern-eating feline," he said.

She pressed her lips together. Sighed softly. Her hands lifted and pressed against his chest for the briefest of moments before she gasped and yanked them away, tucking them behind her back as if she'd done something wrong.

He could still feel the imprint of that brief touch just as vividly as he could feel the cat-scratch stinging from the alcohol. He ran his thumb along her cheek. Cupped his hand over her shoulder, feeling the supple skin through her robe. "I'm sorry about the reporter. I thought the press would've lost interest in me years ago."

"It's not your fault."

"And you're too generous." He settled his thumb on the center of her lower lip, watching her eyelids flicker, then fall. Heard her catch her breath. She'd be generous in bed, too. The sure knowledge dragged at him.

He gently pressed with his thumb and her lips

parted. Her hand closed over his forearm. He lowered his head toward hers, absorbing the scent of her, the warmth.

The ringing.

She gasped and scurried away into the kitchen to grab the ringing telephone.

Tris gritted his teeth, pressing his hands against the wall. He was a dog. Every bit as bad as the news stories slyly implied. He beat down the fire in his gut that urged him to go after her, to take the phone off the hook and to sweep her down the hall to the bedroom he could see at the end.

A bedroom with a narrow, girlish bed, complete with a big, worn, stuffed rabbit sitting against the ruffled, pink pillows.

He silently cursed himself to hell and back. The sight of that bed did what nothing else had been able to do—douse him with cold reality.

He had no business seeking her out in the middle of the night. She was a hometown girl with "innocent" all but tattooed on her forehead, and he was leaving town again after the wedding, in just a few days.

She was sitting at the table, obviously finished with her phone call, when he went into the kitchen again. She just stared at him.

"I should go."

She nodded.

He left the way he'd come—through the back kitchen door. When he stepped out onto the little porch, his wet shirt clung to his chest, cold though the night air was still warm. A lover's-night warmth.

He stood there, on the outside of the door, feeling her on the other side. He slowly buttoned the shirt.

After a long while, he heard the lock click into place behind him.

He sighed. And walked away.

Chapter Six

"What did you do to that girl?"

Tris barely heard Sawyer's demanding question. He was too busy following Hope out the door of the sheriff's office. She'd arrived not two seconds earlier to deliver Sawyer's lunch order from the café. But the sight of Tris, sitting there working on Sawyer's computer, had turned her right around on her heels, barely taking time to drop the brown bag of food onto the straight-back chair just inside the door.

He stepped out onto the sidewalk just in time to see the end of her braid streaming behind her as she darted into the café a few doors down.

"Think before you run after her," Sawyer cautioned, joining him. "Every time you even *look* in the direction of the café, you send the grapevine into apoplexy." He shook his head. "Wish you'd turn off the love 'em and leave 'em mentality for just one week. She's got to stay here when you're gone. Is it worth a few hours of tangled sheets?''

Tris had felt like sludge ever since he'd heard Hope turn the kitchen lock on him last night. He'd also heard plenty that morning at breakfast because he'd missed the end of the bachelor party and had ended up hitching a ride back to the ranch. He didn't need to hear that another family member thought he'd seduced Hope.

Not one of them knew what was going on between them. What *wasn't* going on between them.

Ignoring Sawyer, he started down the sidewalk. When he entered the café, he felt at least a dozen pairs of eyes staring him down. He focused on Ruby, standing behind the counter, her short, white curls practically vibrating off her head as she furiously scrubbed the counter. There was no welcome in her bright eyes. None at all.

All conversations had ceased. Tristan's footsteps sounded loud as he crossed the floor. "I want to talk to Hope," he said to Ruby when he reached the counter.

Her aging, wrinkled face tightened. "What for?"

Hell. He didn't want to upset Ruby. She was part of his childhood. Coming to the café for her delicious pecan-crusted cinnamon rolls; chocolate malts that were so thick you couldn't suck the ice cream drink through a straw; handing over his report cards when she demanded to see them on report card day. "Ruby," he said quietly. "You know I don't want her hurt, either."

Her lips tightened. But he could see in her eyes

that she was softening. "She'll be with me at the wedding," she said. "You can see her, then."

"Gram."

Tris looked over to see Hope standing in the swinging door that led to the kitchen.

Ruby huffed and tossed up her hands. As soon as the swinging door closed, with Tris and Hope in the empty kitchen, he heard a half-dozen conversations start up again out in the dining area.

He pushed his hands into the pockets of his jeans. "Why did you run out of the office like that?"

"Because I'm a fool," she said. "But you shouldn't have followed me."

"You know," he mused softly, "I've never much been one for following the expectations of others. If I had been, I wouldn't have struck out on my own at eighteen with nothing but determination and dreams swimming in my head. Why did you run out like that? Are you upset about last night?"

She wouldn't look at him and he couldn't believe the wave of frustration that buffeted him. "Dammit, Hope, what is it? Don't you know by now that you can talk to me?"

"Tristan, please, you should go. Just trust me. Go."

"Look, I'm sorry about the ruckus over our…friendship…but I'll be damned if I'll let a bunch of gossips dictate my actions. I thought you felt the same. That's why you refused to hide out at the Double-C until I leave town again."

Her eyes wouldn't meet his. "I was talking then about that reporter. *Her* stories—" Her voice shook, but when Tris started toward her, she held up a hand, her expression pleading. "—not about my own friends and family."

"People who should know you better than that."

"You just don't understand," she whispered.

"Then help me to!"

Her lips pressed together. "Your reputation is already settled in gold," she began, clearing her throat, but her voice was still husky. "People think you're larger than life. The more supermodels you dated, the better. The more money you earned, the happier people here were. You're admired as much for the things people whisper about behind their hands as you are criticized. It's not the same for me."

His hands curled. "I'm just a guy, Hope. It shouldn't be any different for me than it is for you."

"Calling you 'just a guy' is like calling the Double-C a little cow kennel. Just stop, would you?" Her eyes pleaded. "Maybe you feel some…passing fancy for me, but I know just as well as everyone else in this town that *that* is all it is. Maybe you're so hung up over your daddy's wedding that you're desperate for some diversion, but I can't be it! Not anymore."

"I'm not 'hung up' over Squire's wedding," he denied flatly. "And maybe I'm used to…having women in my life. But the women in my life are just that. Women. Who expect as little from me as I expect from them."

Hope's lips parted. "That's horrible."

"That's life, sweet pea. My life, anyway. And maybe I want to kiss you more than is wise—hell, I *know* I want to—but I can control myself, which

I'd think you'd know after last night. You don't have to run away from me like I'm ready to jump your bones at the first opportunity, regardless of our surroundings.''

''I don't!''

''What was that about at Sawyer's office, then?''

''Bennett Ludlow's office is next door to the sheriff's office,'' she finally said, as if pushed beyond endurance. ''And frankly, if I want to keep my job, I don't want him seeing you and me within the same *block* of one another.''

''Bennett is a jerk. He always has been.''

''He controls my career. Which he reminded me of very clearly last night when he called!''

Anger curled darkly through him. ''That was Bennett on the phone last night?''

She turned her back on him, pressing her palms against a stainless steel table, and nodded.

''He often call you in the middle of the night?''

''As often as you visit.''

He deserved that, and a part of him applauded her for saying it, even if it stung. But, God, if Tris was too old for Hope, then Bennett was even worse. The guy was old enough to be her father. ''What did he want?'' The last he'd seen, Bennett had been at the bachelor party.

She didn't look at him. ''To tell me that he's called a school board meeting for Monday morning.''

''Why?''

''To fire me, I suppose.''

He stilled. She was too calm.

''On what grounds?''

"Moral misconduct."

He walked over to her. Physically turned her around to face him. "Excuse me?"

"It's in my teaching contract," she said flatly. But her eyes shimmered with tears.

"You haven't done anything!" Not with him and damn sure not with anyone else.

"That doesn't really matter, does it? Everyone thinks I have. The news people think I'm your latest…lover. Gram is afraid I've fallen into my mother's footsteps. The school board, Bennett included, thinks I'm c-carrying on inappropriately. You know, my mother and Justine had to move away from Weaver when Justine was in high school because she was supposedly having an affair with an older man. But nobody ever seemed to blame the guy, whoever he was. They just considered my sister a tramp and that was that."

"That was years ago, Hope."

"Yes," she agreed. "But memories are long in this town, and I grew up hearing the stories."

He swore.

She closed her eyes. "Please, Tristan. Just go now."

She looked fragile and young and frightened. "I'll make this right, Hope," he promised. Anything to take that look off her face.

"You can't. There is nothing to be done."

"So you're just going to let them fire you. With no cause. You're just going to give up."

"What would you have me do?"

"Fight them!"

"With what?" She stared at her hands. "I'm a

Leoni, Tristan. It wouldn't matter if I became a nun, there would still be people in this town who would believe, simply because of my mother and sister, that I was seducing the priests!''

''All this because I carried you down the street?''

''All this because Bennett saw you at my house last night. It was late and you were half-naked, to use his words, and I wasn't exactly wearing jeans and sweatshirt, either.'' She wearily pressed her palm to her forehead. ''On top of everything else…''

''He's not going to fire you.''

''You can't stop him, Tristan. You're not even a resident here, anymore. And your family, as…well, as influential as they are, none of them sits on the board, either. This is my own battle.''

''Which you won't fight!'' He shook her gently. ''This is ridiculous. Tell them to shove it where the sun doesn't shine. You can move somewhere else, have some freedom to live without the people around you judging you. I'll help you find something.''

''I don't want to move somewhere else.''

He realized she meant it. He could see it in her swimming eyes and he felt even more like pond scum.

''I might have been born in Colorado, but Weaver is my home,'' Hope said shakily. ''And I love it here. My Gram, she's been everything to me. I don't even remember my own mother, except for the photographs Gram has and the ring I wear on my necklace. I have friends here. People who care about me. People *I* care about. The ones who are gossiping…they don't mean to be hurtful. They just…this is a small town. Everything that happens here seems to carry more importance or more significance than it would elsewhere. You live in California, and people probably don't bat an eye at the women who come and go through your front door. But here, it's different.''

The tears had slipped over her lashes and the sight twisted his guts into knots. He didn't even bother correcting her assumption that he had a revolving door where women were concerned. ''I'll talk to Bennett.''

She smiled sadly, dashing a hand across her cheek. ''He can be decent enough when he wants, but we all know he has a grudge against anyone with the last name of Clay. Your talking to him wouldn't help. But I appreciate the gesture.''

She appreciated his gesture. The politeness knifed through his soul like a hot poker. He tugged her closer and folded his arms around her shoulders. She was so stiff he could have snapped her into two brittle pieces. Then suddenly, she drew in a breath that shuddered through them both.

''It's such a mess,'' she said against his chest.

He pressed his lips to the top of her hair. ''I'll figure something out, sweet pea. I started it, and I will stop it.'' He thought briefly of the case he'd cleaned up before he'd arrived in Weaver. It had taken nearly a week to untangle the mess an associate had made, but he'd succeeded. Hell, he always succeeded.

Despite the fact that he considered Hope's options far more open than she did when it came to Weaver and her teaching position, it was now his *own* mess to clean up. He'd start by untangling the web of gossip one strand at a time until Hope's reputation was as pristine as ever.

And he'd have to do it before Bennett's damned meeting on Monday morning.

* * *

"Gracious, he *is* a handsome one. It's no wonder people talk about him so much. When he was a boy he was impossible to resist. So sad he never had a chance to know his mama. She was a real lady. Never said an unkind word about anyone."

Hope was climbing from the car and nearly dropped her keys, she was so surprised. "You haven't said one nice thing about Tristan in days," Hope murmured, looking at her grandmother across the roof of the car. Her grandmother who had insisted that she come to this wedding, no matter what. Her grandmother who had pushed a lace dress into Hope's hands and insisted that if she hadn't done anything wrong, as she claimed, then she couldn't avoid the wedding by acting as if she were ashamed.

Gram patted her fresh curls and adjusted her white purse over her elbow. "He's not all bad. And you do like him, don't you?"

Hope closed the car door, not answering. Most of the town was expected to turn out at the Double-C ranch to attend Squire Clay's wedding to Gloria Day. Hope would have avoided it altogether if not for Gram's insistence that if Hope didn't attend, Gram wouldn't either. It was emotional blackmail, but it was effective. Ruby had known Squire for years. Naturally, she wanted to be present for the wedding.

So Hope had donned her grandmother's antique dress, knowing that Gram had presented it purely as a bribe, since she knew how much Hope loved her old dresses. And she'd driven them out to the ranch with the specific intention of avoiding Tristan Clay at all costs.

Only there he was. Standing by the corner of the big, imposing house. Perhaps it was the lilac bushes behind him, vivid with lush blooms and glossy leaves that made his black tuxedo seem even blacker. And perhaps it was the black fabric that fit him like he'd been born to it that made his hair look even brighter, even more gilded.

All she knew was the sight of him made her feet simply take root in the gravel beneath her.

There were dozens of cars already parked in the drive and it was some distance to the house; yet Tristan turned his gaze unerringly in her direction.

Hope blindly shut her car door when her grandmother crunched around the car to tuck her hand through Hope's arm. "Let's go, girl. The chairs are filling, and I want to get a good seat. You know, I heard that Gloria's dress comes all the way from London, England. Have you ever heard such a thing? We've got dressmakers right here in Wyoming. That Squire always did spoil his women. Hard on his sons, but, gracious, he loved his wife. And I haven't seen anything quite as sweet as him, good-looking coot that he is, courting Gloria.

"Sure is nice and tidy that Gloria is working here in town now with Dr. Rebecca. We're getting right metropolitan with a doctor and a nurse. Gloria called me last week, you know. To make sure I'd made that appointment with Dr. Rebecca.''

"Did you?" Hope murmured absently. But her grandmother's chatter was effective, allowing Hope the willpower to drag her gaze from Tristan to look at the rows and rows of white chairs that had been set out on the front lawn. Swags of airy white tulle swayed in the faint breeze, and lilacs and white daisies festooned the chair at the end of each row. A good portion of the seats were already occupied, and those that weren't soon would be, once the clusters of standing guests seated themselves.

"Next Wednesday," Ruby replied as they luckily found two seats near the front. Hope folded her hands in her lap, absently listening to Ruby chatter to the guests around them, as naturally as if the craziness of the last week had never occurred. Maybe it hadn't. Maybe Hope had built it up in her mind to be worse than it really was.

Or maybe it was just that her grandmother had had plenty of practice at holding her head up when other people were gossiping about her family.

Hope tucked her keys in her tiny, useless purse that held only a minimum of essentials and smoothed the dress over her knees. At least the chairs faced away from the house, she thought. Away from Tristan.

Bennett and the two other members of the school board stood on the far side of the chairs on the other side of the aisle. She felt her face burn, knowing they were watching her.

Jolie and Drew and little Evan Taggart arrived,

and Hope felt herself relax a little. Evan hugged her enthusiastically before his daddy nudged him into a chair. Jolie, who looked as bright as a sunflower in her yellow dress, slipped into the seat beside Hope and leaned close. "You've been busy, my friend. I've been trying to call you since Wednesday."

Hope shook her head. "I wasn't answering my phone."

"That awful cousin of Brenda's, I suppose," Jolie finished sympathetically. "I heard she was gonna get fired or transferred or something from her station over the stories she's been telling." She looked around again and leaned close. "So, is it true? Were you really caught doing the horizontal mamba with Tristan during his daddy's bachelor party?"

Hope stared. "What?"

"I knew it couldn't be." Jolie patted her arm.

"That's what people are saying?" She glanced at her grandmother, praying that Gram hadn't heard *that* particular rumor. She leaned toward Jolie. "Who told you that?" she hissed.

Jolie shook her head. "Half-a-dozen people, at least. I told them they were all crazy."

Hope pressed shaking fingers to her lips. She wished more than ever that she'd stayed home.

"Excuse me, Jolie. Hope? I need to talk to you for a minute."

Hope's hands knotted. She looked up at Tristan, who was leaning over, one hand extended to her. *Horizontal mamba.* Please, God, let him not have heard that. Painfully aware of Bennett and his companions watching, Hope shook her head.

"It's important," he said, when Ruby turned and

saw him. "There's not a lot of time before the ceremony begins."

Hope knew that if she dared to look around, she'd find everyone's attention focused on them. Staring. Waiting. Probably thinking she'd throw herself uncontrollably at Tristan in a fit of passion that, as a Leoni, she'd be unable to contain.

"Perhaps you should, girl," Gram patted her hand.

Thoroughly rattled, Hope looked at her grandmother. "Gram—"

"You're a good girl," Gram said softly. "It'll be all right."

Hope looked from her grandmother to Tristan. His face was expressionless except for the muscle ticking in his jaw. He was angry, Hope realized with a start. She was mortified, and he was angry. She moistened her lips and rose. She didn't take his hand, however, and his lips thinned.

He stepped out of the row and waited for her, then tucked his hand at the small of her back; right below the small gathered bow at the center of the scooped back. She felt the grazing contact right down to her toes.

But when he started toward the house, Hope shook her head violently. "We can talk out here."

"Fine." But still, he took her elbow and walked along the side of the house, well away from the gathering guests. "Why didn't you tell me about Bennett's plans to close the school?"

Hope's stomach dropped. "I didn't think about it."

"Bull," he said smoothly. So smoothly and

fiercely that shivers danced over her skin. "You were thinking about it all along. *That* is why you are so afraid of losing your job. Because if the school loses another teacher, Bennett and his side-kicks can close it. The kids will have to be bused to Braden, thirty miles away."

Hope didn't reply. He'd obviously learned the full facts from someone.

He pushed one hand in his pocket. "I can't believe you would just sit back and let Bennett do this."

"I wasn't going to just sit back," she blurted tightly. She'd been doing nothing but worrying and thinking and planning since Bennett's middle-of-the-night call. "But until I can meet with the board the day after tomorrow, I won't even have an opportunity to defend myself officially against their charges."

"What were you planning to do then? Lay yourself across the conference table as a sacrificial lamb, begging their mercy for committing whatever sins they've come up with in their tiny, judgmental minds?"

"Once you're gone, things will die down." She hoped that was the case, anyway. "I'll move back in with my grandmother, if it becomes necessary. And if worse comes to worse, I've called a friend from college who may be willing to move here for a year and apply for my job. If she agrees, hopefully the board would hire her and the school can remain open." It wasn't the best of plans, but it was the only thing she'd been able to come up with.

"Bennett is not going to hire anyone," Tris countered flatly. "He's so mired in paperwork trying to bring about the consolidation of the two schools in Weaver and Braden that I'm not sure he could stop it if he wanted to."

She paused, unease making her queasy. "How do you know that?"

"I made it my business to know. Given opportunity, Bennett's going to pounce." Tris looked over his shoulder at the man in question. Bennett was watching, his expression unreadable at the distance. "The rub is that the board is within its rights to act. Not about firing you because of this moral sh—stuff. But closing the school. Weaver has the students and Braden has the teachers, but Braden's facility is nearly brand new, top of the line, so the argument is that our kids will benefit more by going there, than shuffling *them* here."

Hope chewed her lip. Nodded.

"And thanks to my…association with you, he figures he's got the momentum now to push it over the hump."

"If it hadn't been this," she waved her hand, since there weren't any words adequate enough to describe the absurdity, "it would have been something else. Some other teacher he took to task, some reason to close our doors."

"We need to clear your name."

Hope shook her head. "I'm not worried about that. I'm worried about my kids in the fall."

"I figured." He drew his hand out of his pocket and held it out. "This will shut their mouths. If not for good, then at least long enough to give me some breathing room to stop Bennett's plan."

She looked at the square black jeweler's box sitting on the palm of his hand. "I don't understand."

"We're getting married."

Her jaw loosened.

Tristan's thumb flipped open the box and the diamond rings inside glinted whitely under the sunlight. "Once you're my wife, no one will have any cause to speak ill of you. And Bennett can take his morals and shove 'em u—"

"No!" She reached for the box and snapped it shut. Hiding the impossibly beautiful rings from sight.

"Yes. We will do this. Here. Today."

"Your father is getting married today!" She frowned up at him. "Are you drunk again?"

"Sweet pea, I've never been more sober in my life."

"But you don't love me!"

She caught something in his eyes. Something sad. "It's the only way I can right what's wrong," he said. His impassive voice held none of the fleeting expression she'd thought she'd glimpsed in his eyes.

"Is that so important?"

He rubbed his thumb over the box. "It's what I do, Hope. And I won't let you, or the kids who go to school here suffer because I didn't think beyond my—because I thought flirting with a very pretty, sweet young woman would be harmless."

She *wasn't* pretty. And still, Tristan stood in front of her, a jeweler's box in his hand, expecting her to marry him. To protect her. Her chest filled with panic and too many emotions to name. But mostly panic. Oh, yes. Panic. "People would know it was only for show,'' she pointed out, struggling for breath. ''You...you said you were going to France after the wedding. And I would still be here. That would be just one more thing with which they'd take exception. It may seem quaint and old fashioned to you, but I do think this area of the world expects wives to live *with* their husbands... Gads, I can't believe I'm even discussing this. It's crazy.''

''It's the perfect answer. And you can come to Paris with me. Once my work there is done, we'll go to my place in California. You can spend the rest of the summer there. I've got a number of social engagements that I can't get out of. You can go with me, or just lay around on the beach or by the pool. Whatever. Then, if you still want to teach here in Weaver, you can come back in the fall. Or arrange for your friend to come, after all. Either way, Bennett will have a hard time pushing through the school closure. He'll have a full roster of teachers again, and the funding is still in place.''

''Of course I still want to teach at the school. It's all I've wanted since I was six years old, attending first grade there myself!''

''That's your choice.'' There was a fine white line surrounding his mobile lips. ''I realize I'm no prize, but as my wife, your options *will* be open, Hope.''

As his wife. Wife. ''No.'' She shook her head violently. Not a prize? That was proof that this wasn't really happening. ''I have to join my grandmother, now. Everybody is sitting down, and the minister is over there waiting with your father and brothers. We're attracting too much attention.''

He caught her hand in a gentle, inescapable grip. "Hope."

She drew in a panicky breath, feeling desperately close to tears. "We can't get married. We can't. We...uh, we...we don't have a license!"

He tucked his other hand inside his lapel and drew out a folded sheet. "I called in a few favors," he said, handing it to her.

Hope twisted her hand free and unfolded the document. It was *her* name typed on the license. *His* name. And it was signed and stamped and looked utterly official. "No."

"It's the only way, Hope."

She pushed the wedding license back into his hand and curled her fingers into a fist, as if by doing so she could prevent him from sliding that theoretical ring onto her finger.

Only this wasn't theoretical. It *was* happening, and it was very, very real.

Beyond Tristan's shoulder she could see the string quartet set up off to the side of the white chairs; could hear the lilting strains floating on the afternoon breeze. The groom and Tristan's brothers were all lined up, too, obviously waiting for him before they moved to the head of the aisle and awaited the arrival of the bride.

She thought about the day of Gloria's wedding shower and the little girls she'd watched. Of Evan. They were only a few of the children who would have to be bused thirty miles beyond Weaver to a school that offered every physical advantage, but was still miles away from their own home.

Once the school closed, Hope knew it was unlikely that it would reopen. Weaver would begin to die away, just like so many other small towns died away when their young ones grew up and left. Never to return.

"What will Gram think?"

His expression didn't change one iota, but she knew. "Oh my! Gram knows, doesn't she? That's why she insisted I come today." She flicked her ankle-length skirt. "And this dress."

He didn't deny it. "Marry me. Right here. Right now."

Barely able to breathe, she stared at Tristan's outstretched palm. A million thoughts whirled through her mind. The clipping inside her old geometry book. The tiredness in Tristan's eyes the first day when he'd appeared in the café and the amusement that day in the park. The Chinese food cartons he'd stuck in her hands the night she was watching Evan.

She pressed her hand to her head, feeling dizzy from the thoughts. Or maybe it was just his presence that made her dizzy.

Not certain she'd ever draw a sane breath again, Hope placed her shaking hand in his. "All right," she whispered, "I'll marry you."

Chapter Seven

Squire and Gloria hadn't planned to share their wedding day. But when Tris escorted Hope through the back of the big house, tugging her unresistingly into the living room where his future stepmother and a bevy of excited women waited, he had to admit that Gloria accepted the news with typical equanimity, though he received some strongly shocked looks from his sisters-in-law.

But he couldn't worry about what they thought. Getting Hope through the ceremony and her signature on the license afterward was his focus. There'd been another way to stop Bennett, but after speaking with Ruby that morning, Tris couldn't bring himself to do it. Marrying Hope was the far easier thing to do. He'd been honest when he'd told her that they'd figure out the rest later.

Seeing that Hope, pale and shaky, was being capably taken under the wings of the other women as they rearranged floral bouquets and such, he headed out the front door and down one side of the two-hundred white chairs. He joined the men and met the minister's eyes.

The other man nodded imperceptibly at the string quartet, and the guests suddenly hushed.

Tris was aware of the close look he received from Squire when he moved next to him, where Sawyer—as best man—had been designated to stand. But he ignored his father and concentrated on the opened doorway of the big house.

His nieces all came first, looking like cherubs in white and yellow ruffles as they solemnly dropped their flower petals from their matching baskets along the way. Then Maggie and Emily and Jaimie came out of the doorway, stepping gracefully down the steps, followed by Rebecca, who was Gloria's boss now, as well as her friend.

And finally, Hope appeared. Even across the yards, her eyes focused on his and with every fiber inside him, Tris willed her to walk surely down the aisle. To hold her head up, because she hadn't done one damned thing wrong—was in fact so good inside that she was marrying a man who was nowhere near as good as she in order to save something far more important than just a job.

He watched, impassive, as Hope moved forward. She looked lovely with her thick hair twisted at her nape and that old-fashioned-looking dress barely skimming her curves like some movie star of the twenties. But the only thing similar to the other women in the wedding party was the cluster of flowers she carried in her hands.

She did walk gracefully down the steps of the big house. And she did walk up the aisle with no shred of nervousness showing, except maybe the trembling of the flowers in her hands.

He stepped forward, meeting her part way along the aisle to tuck her shaking hand around his arm where no one could see and she looked at him with eyes glazed by panic.

Because of what people would think or say? Or because she knew somewhere inside her that she was marrying a man who would never love her?

He walked her the rest of the way, to stand beside his father and heard the collective gasp of the guests as it began to dawn on them what they were seeing, when she didn't move off to the side as the other women had done.

He ignored the avidly curious looks he knew they were receiving. And he ignored the "good thing you're doing right by that girl," his father grunted in his ear.

The guests didn't know whether to stare at the sight of Tristan and Hope, or enjoy the lovely picture Gloria made as she glided down the aisle after her daughters, Belle and Nikki. Gloria's dress was violet in color, Tris noticed, thinking the color matched Hope's eyes.

Then, Gloria joined Squire, and the four of them turned to face the minister.

"Dearly Beloved," he began.

"And to the bride and groom—*both* sets of them—may they have as much happiness and love in their lives always as they do today.''

Hope listened to Sawyer Clay's toast with disbelief. Tristan had pushed a crystal flute of champagne into her hands several minutes ago and she'd
already drained it. A white-coated waiter had immediately replaced it with a full one. As if it were
against the rules for the bride—either one of them—
to be seen without a full champagne glass in her
hand.

She smiled and murmured nonsensically at the
stream of people who passed by offering well wishes
and expressions of surprise. Even Bennett managed
a tight smile when he lightly kissed her cheek and
briefly shook Tristan's hand before moving on to
Gloria and Squire. Tristan leaned down to murmur
in Hope's ear, ''If I didn't know better, I'd say he
looked almost relieved.''

Hope dragged her thoughts from the ceremony
that had passed in a blur. Except for the moment
when Tristan slid the perfectly fitted wedding set on
her finger. That was perfectly clear in her thoughts.
The way he'd lowered his head over hers and
pressed an impossibly gentle, but much too brief,
kiss on her lips was even more clear. She frowned
up at Tristan, his question finally sinking in. She
swayed a little at finding him standing so close.
''Who?''

''Bennett,'' he said.

''Frustrated at being thwarted is more like it,''
Hope dismissed. ''Assuming this plan actually suc-
ceeds.'' She turned blindly to receive the next
guest's best wishes.

It seemed to take an interminable amount of time for all the guests to make their way along the receiving line. But Hope realized about halfway through that the more champagne she drank, the easier it became. That, plus the steady wall Tristan made beside her as he kept her tucked close against him. She wasn't even aware of leaning against him, letting him take more of her weight, until he slipped the champagne flute out of her hand and set it on the tray of a passing waiter.

"Enough for you, I think," he murmured. "Come on. We have to cut a piece of cake, dance a time or two, then we can get out of here."

They headed toward the cake table, where another ribbon-bedecked cake knife had appeared to join the first. They cut and fed each other a morsel and smiled dutifully and even laughed at the toasts directed at Squire and Gloria and at them.

And when the sun was starting to drop toward the horizon, the string quartet was replaced by a live band and the dancing began.

Closing her eyes, pressing her cheek against Tristan's chest, Hope could almost make herself believe that it all was real. That she'd married the man of her dreams, that he'd married her because he couldn't bear to live his life without her.

"But it's not like that," she murmured sleepily. Not for her mother, not for Justine, not for her.

"What's not?"

She blinked up at Tristan, focusing until she saw only one of him. "You did plan this with Gram, didn't you. She told you about the school."

"Yes."

"She says you'll break my heart." Hope heard the words come out of her mouth with a kind of fascinated, dulled horror. "But today she said you always were hard to resist. She's almost always right."

Tristan pressed his hand gently against her head. "Stop worrying."

"Okay." She closed her eyes and listened to the swaying beat of the mournful love song. He danced beautifully. He did everything beautifully. Even rescuing the abruptly tarnished reputation of the plain, hometown girl.

"May I?"

Hope craned her neck around to see Squire Clay waiting to cut in. Before she could blink, Tristan had surrendered her to his father—her father-in-law, she realized with panic—and was now dancing with Gloria.

"I won't bite you, child." Squire took her hands and simply began guiding her around in an easy waltz, since she seemed incapable of moving on her own.

Hope started to speak, but didn't know what on earth to say. Had he heard all the gossip, too? It seemed likely. "I'm sorry." The words burst from her.

His pale, ice-blue eyes were sharp, but not unkind. "For loving my son?"

"I—" What could she say?

"You do, don't you?"

She moistened her lips. "I, um, I married him," she said weakly.

Squire turned her in a slow circle and her head

swam dizzily. "He sure in he…sure did surprise us all. Too bad he didn't give me a clue what he'd planned. His mama had a cameo that she wore on our wedding day. Would'a looked right nice on your dress today. Passed on from her grandmother—last name was Tristan."

If his easy tone was meant to relax, it was failing miserably. Hope concentrated on the studs of the man's shirt. He wasn't quite as tall as his youngest son, but he was still nearly as broad in the shoulder and made an intimidating, imposing sight. "I imagine you expected more for him," she said shakily.

"More?"

"Someone more, ah, suitable."

He smiled slightly, reminding her strongly of Tristan. "I believe he's made the perfect match. Just like his old man has."

Hope blushed. If only that were true. They circled the dance area marked off by the twinkling lights a few more times, then Hope found herself with more champagne and more dancing with each one of Tristan's brothers.

They were an intense lot, but as quietly kind as Squire had been. Nevertheless, Hope was impossibly relieved when she wound up with Tristan once again. So relieved that she unknowingly curled her fingers into his collar and rested her head on his wide chest.

"You've charmed my family," he murmured. "I've been getting warnings from all sides to treat you right."

Hope focused on his words. "You really didn't tell them, then. The real reason?"

"It's nobody's business but our own," he said shortly. He whirled her in a smooth circle, bending her over his arm with a flourish as the song died.

Her head spun when he straightened. "Oh my."

His arm around her shoulders held her upright. "Flattering to know you have to get tanked to get through this," he murmured in her ear.

She made a face. "I like that champagne. I've never had you—*it*, I mean—before, you know."

"I figured."

The music began again. Low and slow and yearning. More couples crowded into the area between the round banquet-style tables. Hope's senses swam. "You smell good."

"You smell good, too," he murmured. "But remind me never to let you have more than one glass of champagne again."

"Okay." She breathed the word. Somehow or other, her hand had reached the back of his neck and she pushed her fingertips luxuriously through his hair. It felt as wonderfully thick and silky as it looked.

"Behave yourself," he murmured.

"I always behave myself." She suddenly had to enunciate carefully. "That's what I do. You're a protect-or. I'm a behave-er."

She felt his chest rumble with a soft chuckle. And for the first time in what seemed like days, she smiled, too. Because dancing with Tristan really was an experience she'd never thought she'd have. And it was one that she intended to tuck away in her heart to relive later on.

Once Tristan returned to his world and she was

left in hers, everything would be normal once again. That was when she'd remember the feel of his fine tuxedo jacket under her cheek and the heavy beat of his heart underneath that. When she'd think about the stars that had begun to shine overhead and the romantic sounds from the band, and the champagne that bubbled giddily in her veins.

When things were normal once again. When she was just plain old Hope Leoni, kindergarten-through-third-grade teacher. And this wedding stuff was just a dream.

It wasn't a dream.

Hope leaned across the carpeted aisle of the jet, took her eyeglasses from Tristan and shoved them in place. Moving too fast made her dizzy, though, and she cursed the champagne that several hours earlier she'd blessed.

"We'll get an annulment," she said abruptly. It didn't matter that Tristan seemed to believe they'd done the right thing in wedding one another—that by doing so, her reputation was protected and the school was out of danger for now. She must have been out of her mind to agree.

Tristan had leaned back in his high-backed, leather chair and his head was no longer within the circle of light cast by the lamp on the table beside him. "No."

Her hair was everywhere. She yanked it over one shoulder and roughly braided it. But she didn't have anything to fasten the end. Goodness knows what happened to the hair pins she'd used earlier to anchor her chignon. She braided anyway. Then left it hanging over her shoulder. "We have to."

"Why?"

"Because it was madness for us to resort to this in the first place!" She winced at the way her raised voice resonated unpleasantly inside her skull.

"You don't have much of a head for champagne."

"I don't have *any* head at all when it comes to you," she muttered. "Oh, Tristan, *what* have we done?"

"I could explain again," he said dryly, "but I think we've beat that one to death already."

She pushed to her feet, swaying for a moment. "I can't believe you'd joke at a time like this."

"Meet the real Tris Clay." He propped one foot on his knee. "Nice enough until you get to know him. Then, you find out he's all surface and no substance."

Hope blinked. "More jokes." She folded her arms and started pacing. She pressed her fingertips to her forehead. "Where are we going?"

"Paris, sweet pea. How much *do* you remember, anyway?"

Her restless pacing stopped. "I don't even have a passport!"

"Taken care of."

She peered at his shadowed face. "Excuse me? Don't you need, I don't know, my birth certificate and photo and…and stuff?"

He nodded.

Her lips parted. She couldn't think what to say.

She wasn't even sure she *had* a copy of her birth certificate— "Gram," she realized aloud.

The plane hit a bump, and she swallowed an abrupt surge of nausea that made her completely forget everything. She pressed her palm flat against her tummy, biting her lip. Tristan rose, saying something unrepeatable under his breath, and hooking his arm around her waist, hauled her along the plane. Toward the rear? She didn't know, didn't care, because he pushed open a door and nudged her inside and at the sight of the commode, Hope slammed the door shut in his face and lost her lunch.

She washed her face and sat weakly on the edge of the bathtub. A bathtub on a plane? She stared at it as if she expected it to disappear. But it didn't. It stayed right there, solid as could be underneath her rear.

It was so ridiculous, as ridiculous as this whole situation. She didn't know whether to laugh or cry.

But the tears clouding her vision told her the decision for that had already been made.

She sucked in a hard breath, scrubbing furiously at her cheeks. She might be shy, but she wasn't a cry baby. And she *had* agreed to marry Tristan. It wasn't as if he'd held a gun to her head and forced her to say "I do."

If anything, he'd been remarkably sweet. In a…a forceful kind of way.

The idiocy of that had her rising to her feet. She splashed cool water over her face and reached for the velvety thick towel hanging on a gold bar beside the sink. Her fingers pressed into the ivory thickness. She'd never seen a towel so outlandishly plush.

Shaking her head gingerly, she dried her face and hands and carefully hung the towel back exactly as it had been. Then she swallowed and pulled open the door, breathing a little easier when she didn't find Tristan hovering outside.

He—or someone—had turned on some very low music. The plane was enormous, she realized, as she slowly padded back along the hall. Her own little house would have easily fit inside it. There was even a staircase leading up to another floor. Floor? She swallowed and peered up the curving metal staircase, but she couldn't see anything up there. Just thick shadows interspersed with an odd, greenish glow.

A low murmur drew her along the hall. When she rounded a curve in the interior wall before the hall widened into the same area where she'd awakened, she realized that Tristan was talking on a phone.

He was sitting in that same big, leather chair. Only this time he didn't look relaxed and amused. She hovered in the hallway. He sat with his elbows on his thighs, one hand shoving through his gilded hair and the other clenching a phone to his ear. He seemed to be staring at the floor between his squarely planted, polished boots.

Even his shoulders looked weary.

Hope quietly backed along the hallway, and slid down that odd, curving interior wall until she sat on the floor. She stared down at her dress—the beautiful lace dress that was the color of dairy cream tinted by coffee. She had told Gram the dress was more suitable for Justine's exotic beauty than for her, with its flyaway sleeves and plunging back, but Gram hadn't agreed. Now she knew why.

Hope sighed. She had hadn't had much chance to speak with Gram at the reception. Ruby had left on a promise to take care of Simon, long before Tristan and Hope had finally departed.

Her head ached as she tried to recall the exact details of that departure. Mostly, it was one big blur. She didn't even remember boarding this extraordinary plane.

"…Dom, I know it wasn't in the plan, dammit, but there's nothing I can do about it. I'm bringing a friend, so get used to it. Just make bloody sure to clear the suite. And clear your schedule to take her around the city…yes, you will, because I'm telling you to. Take her sightseeing or something—just keep her busy."

Hope tried to blot out Tristan's voice, but she couldn't. No more than she could forget the sight of him, hunched over like he wanted to tear his hair out by the roots. She drew up her knees and carefully tucked the dress over them. Why couldn't the low music be louder so that it blotted out that roughly impatient voice?

"Has anything ever distracted me from the job? Or *anyone* for that matter? Nothing has changed. Trust me."

Hope lowered her forehead to her knees.

What a mess.

Chapter Eight

White-gold sunlight speared through the tall windows, cutting across the bed with its mound of pillows. The billowy duvet was tangled in a pale blue heap at the foot of the bed, tumbling halfway off the mattress onto the carpet. Hope stood in the doorway of the adjoining bathroom, tightening the belt of the pristine white terry cloth robe she'd found hanging in the closet, and looked at the disheveled bed.

She, alone, was responsible for the bed getting into such a state. If she had thought Tristan had created a whirlwind through their wedding and reception and the flight, it was nothing compared to the rapid activity she'd experienced when they'd landed. Three men had surrounded her and Tristan the moment they stepped off the plane. They'd barely looked sideways at her, but the way they deferred to Tristan was telling.

After a hair-raising car ride, Tristan had hustled her through a discreet side door of an elegant looking hotel and swept her along with him onto an elevator where he'd punched in some sort of code on a keypad on the wall. Then he'd left her alone in this high-ceilinged, sumptuous bedroom.

She didn't have a clue what room he'd left his ragged black duffel in—if he'd even remained in the hotel, that is.

She'd fallen into bed even though the sun was still above the horizon, slept restlessly and risen again to a sun that was bright and full.

"The wedding night of every girl's dreams," she murmured aloud. Not that she wanted anything different, of course. Did she? She was married to a stranger. Was it any wonder that she felt unsettled?

Hungover, she corrected. That's what she was. Pure and simple. The shower hadn't helped. She tucked her wet hair behind her ears and wandered across the acres of carpet. The fact that the pastel toned carpet was comfortably worn didn't detract from the beautiful floral pattern. The tall windows opened onto a small, iron-railed balcony, and she slowly pulled open the doors. Then she stepped out into the sunlight to a view of a formal garden that was so beautiful she could have looked at it for hours.

The garden was idyllic, but the noise hovering in the air was anything but. Cars. Lots and lots of cars going every which way with no discernable pattern.

She sighed and folded her arms on the rail, tuning

out the cacophony. She suspected it was late morning, but her internal clock was so discombobulated she couldn't have sworn to it. What she did know, however, was that she had no desire whatsoever to put on her coffee-tinted lace dress. Yet it was the only item of clothing she had—except for the lone robe that she'd found.

As thoroughly as Tristan had planned for every contingency, he hadn't thought to stop and collect some of her clothes before whisking her off for their "honeymoon." Even her Gram hadn't come up with some sneaky way of doing that.

Her stomach rumbled and she went back inside, reluctantly closing the windows against the view, but it was so much quieter when she did so. She pulled in a deep breath, opened the bedroom door and stuck out her head. "Quiet as a tomb," she muttered. But somewhere there should be a phone, and room service, with any luck. Her high school French lessons seemed a long time ago, but she figured "coffee" was fairly universal.

Maybe, along the way in her search she'd even find the man she'd married.

She stuck her head in one opened door after another. Tristan had called it a "suite," but as far as Hope was concerned, she felt like she was the only person on the entire floor. She found several other bedrooms, all unoccupied and well appointed, though none quite as lavish as the one she'd used.

She didn't find a phone. But she did find a kitchen. A fully equipped kitchen. A fully *occupied* kitchen.

Hope swallowed against the breath that jammed

in her throat and pressed a shaking hand to her stomach. "Well," she said, feeling positively ill, "I seem to have found the kitchen, the phone *and* you."

She watched Tristan slowly turn toward her and the woman he was with—the woman who had been tangling her red-tipped talons through his blond hair until Hope spoke, raised one raven eyebrow. "Plucking them young these days, aren't you, darling?"

Hope's jaw tightened, and she wished that she'd put on Gram's dress after all. Anything would be better than standing there—wet hair, bare feet and shapeless robe—in the presence of this glossed-to-perfection woman.

Her photo probably accompanied the dictionary's description of *chic,* Hope thought despairingly.

"Shut up, Dom." Tristan waved an absent hand at the table where a tray of fresh fruit and pastries sat. If he felt at all odd that Hope had found him with another woman's hands in his hair, he didn't show it by so much as a blink. "Come on in, Hope."

Lovely. *This* was Dom. The Dom who was supposed to make sure Hope stayed busy. She nearly turned around and headed back the way she'd come. But the glint of superiority in the other woman's eyes stopped her and her feet carried her forward, instead, to the seat Tristan had indicated.

"Did you sleep well?" he asked, pulling out one of the other chairs and straddling it.

The words came out before she thought, just as her gaze skimmed once again over that woman. "Did you?"

The woman laughed softly. She smoothed her lily-white hand over Tristan's denim-clad shoulder, and then held it out toward Hope. "I'm Dominique Marchand," she introduced herself in a faintly accented voice. "Welcome to Paris. Tris doesn't usually bring women here. He doesn't have that much sentiment in his soul."

"Enough, Dom."

Hope wondered at the irritation in Tristan's voice. She wanted to shake the woman's hand about as much as she wanted to kiss a snake. A lifetime of Gram's good manners made her do so. But it was brief, and afterward, beneath the cover of the table, Hope smoothed her hand across her robe as if to wipe away the contact.

She also wondered whether Dominique meant Tristan didn't bring women to Paris in general, or didn't bring women *here*. Why would he need to? He obviously had *Dom*. Sentiment or not. And it was clear that he hadn't mentioned their marriage.

Her throat was tight, but the room itself seemed to wait for her response. "Thank you. Is this a hotel, Tristan? It seems more like an apartment building or something."

"A hotel," he said, shooting the other woman a look that Hope couldn't interpret. "But I'm here a lot and keep this floor available for my use year-round." He nudged the platter toward her. "Once you've eaten, you'll probably want to call your grandmother. I've got some work that will keep me busy for quite a while, but there's plenty to entertain you. An indoor pool and the garden in the courtyard. Shops nearby. We're just off the Champs Élysées.

Dom will take you around the city if you want to do some sight—"

"I'm sure I can occupy myself," Hope interrupted. She reached for a croissant, even though her appetite had ground down to nothing, and stood. "You and your friend needn't worry about me." She turned to go.

"Hope, hold on—"

"Let her go, darling, can't you see she's—"

Hope didn't hang around to hear the rest. *"By all means, darling,"* she mimicked under her breath as she strode along one hallway, then another, trying to find her way through the mazelike floor plan to her bedroom. "Working. Right." Finally, she saw the right door.

"Talking to yourself?"

"Oh!" Hope's foot slid on the cold marble floor and she scrambled for balance, dropping the croissant her clenched fingers had smashed. "Where did you come from?"

Tristan smiled faintly and pointed a thumb over his shoulder in the opposite direction. "Through there." He reached down and scooped up the croissant.

Hope yanked the sash of her robe tighter and sidled around him into the bedroom. "Well. Excuse me."

"Not so fast, sweet pea." He prevented her from closing the door with the flat of his hand.

She released the door, backing away toward the tall windows. "It's your hotel...*floor.* What did you do? Buy it?"

"Sort of. Does that bother you?" He stepped into the room and slowly pushed the door closed.

Feeling every bit the ninny she was, Hope shrugged. She wished he'd left the door open. With it shut, with her bed still tumbled from her restless sleep, she felt buffeted by a nagging sense of intimacy that was so far from reality it nearly made her laugh. Or cry. "Not at all," she denied. "I, uh, I thought you had to work."

He left the croissant on the nightstand and brushed off his hands. "I do. What's wrong?"

Everything. She hid her hands in the pockets of her robe. "I think I, um, made a mistake."

"You did?"

"We. We made a mistake." His steady gaze unsettled her. "We *have* to get an annulment."

"No."

"Why not? You surely don't want to be married. I...was weak when I should have stood on my own feet and told Bennett to take a flying leap."

"Bennett will get his," Tristan murmured. "And you're not weak, so stop talking that way. We're married. It's done."

"We, but...we...we don't even know anything about each other! We've never even kissed!" Her cheeks felt on fire. "For...real, I mean."

"Is that an invitation?"

She swallowed and backed away. "No!"

He smiled faintly. "Didn't think so." Then he blew out a slow breath and dropped down onto the foot of her tumbled bed, casually resting his forearms on his thighs. "You're sure now? We *are* married."

Hope frowned severely. That's all she needed. Falling for her husband who apparently had a "Dom" at his beck and call.

"Relax, sweet pea," he said after a moment. "What do you want to know?"

Did Dominique usually use this room? Where had he slept last night? "I don't know!"

He rubbed his jaw, then ran his fingers through his hair. "I'm thirty-four, have all my own teeth and know how to sew a button back on a shirt if it pops off. I'd rather listen to the sound of silence than most any music around, and I hate green beans. Does that help?"

"Don't joke."

"Trust me, sweet pea. The green bean thing is no joke."

She huffed and turned her back on him, escaping onto the small balcony. She stared blindly down at the garden, wishing she had the slightest notion how to handle him.

She wrapped her hands around the rail, and the rings on her finger clinked against it. She wore Clay's wedding band, but she was still a Leoni.

Tristan moved to the rail beside her. "I know this isn't how you expected to spend the rest of your summer," he said quietly, "but if you let yourself, you might enjoy it here. It's Paris."

City of light. City of love. The place where he kept an entire hotel floor available for his use. She stared straight ahead. "Of course."

"Dammit, Hope." He pulled her inexorably around to face him. "Tell me and I'll try to fix it."

"Fixing things is what got us here in the first place."

"So let's make the best of it. I know you've never been to France before. Look at this as a vacation."

"With no clothes?" she burst. "I don't know what kind of vacations *you* take, but I prefer to be dressed on mine! I don't even know how long we're supposed to be here."

He frowned.

"I know you don't pack much—the size of your duffel bag gave that away, but didn't it occur to either you or Gram that I might need something besides that dress?"

He shook his head and nudged her inside. "We didn't have a lot of time to attend to details like that," he said smoothly. "We'll just get some new things for you."

She felt something inside her lift; like a balloon slowly being filled with helium.

"Dom lives to shop. She'll get you fixed up right away."

The helium rushed out with dizzying speed.

"Too bad you're so much taller than she is, or she could give you a few of her things to tide you over while you shop." Now that he apparently figured that all problems were solved, he spoke quickly, as if he'd spent enough of his precious time on this latest little snag.

Hope slowly twisted the rings around her finger. She was only an inch or so taller than Dominique, but the other woman was so excruciatingly thin it would have taken two of her to equal Hope's healthy curves. "So, does Dominique stay here in the hotel, too?"

He nodded, pulling open the door. "Think you can stand wearing your dress for another hour or two?"

Did she have any other choice? "Is this ordinarily her room?"

"What?"

"Dominique. Is this her room?"

"No. Why?"

Hope wished she had enough courage to ask the rest of her question—if Dominique's room was also his room. But she was afraid of the answer. "I didn't want to put anyone out," she said instead. "I'll get dressed now."

He paused for a moment, then nodded again. "Come and find us when you're ready."

Hope shoved her fists into the side pockets of the robe and waited until he'd left, closing the door once more behind him. *Find us.* Just how much of an "us" were he and Dominique?

She wore his rings, though there had never been the slightest discussion about him wearing hers. Had he wanted to wear one, Hope felt sure he wouldn't have overlooked the detail. Which most likely meant the omission was by choice. Instinct had prevented her from offering the one on her necklace—mostly because she couldn't have borne it if—when—he refused it. Even during the wedding ceremony, the minister hadn't looked at Hope as if she was supposed to produce a ring for the man she was impetuously marrying. But what did it matter? What did the rings mean? For her, a cease-fire to the rumors back home in Weaver. But for him? She was merely one more detail in his life about which she knew absolutely nothing.

She was so far out of her depth it scared her. But what scared her more was the depth of her instant dislike for the raven-haired Dominique. And if Tristan thought he could foist her off on Dom, he was dreaming.

That may be the kind of life he led away from Weaver, but she didn't have to accommodate it. The force of her decision left her feeling lightheaded. But at least it was *her* decision.

She straightened her shoulders and strode into the connecting bathroom where she'd left her dress hanging behind the door.

"What do you mean she ditched you?" Tris stared at Dominique.

His associate lifted one impeccable shoulder. "I turned my back for a few moments and she was gone. Poof."

"You're an expert in surveillance," Tris said tightly.

Dominique shrugged again. "Darling, she is a grown woman. She'll find her way back here when she's ready. I still don't know what you brought her here for, anyway. I've got better things to do than babysit your little girlfriend. I'm supposed to be surveilling Pirelli's mistress, not yours. And you've got to break Pirelli's latest computer code so you can do your magic in their databases before Billy and Franco blow their covers and end up dead. We're still behind schedule thanks to Marc." Dominique's obsidian eyes were sharp. "He was thinking about a woman, too."

Marc's mess had nearly gotten Franco—one of Hollins-Winword's best agents since Jefferson's retirement several years earlier—killed once already. It had taken both Coleman Black and Tris to derail that particular disaster without sacrificing eighteen months of work on a case that would put a nasty little terrorist named Abe Pirelli out of illegal arms trading for good. Once they had been satisfied that Franco was safe, Cole had returned to Connecticut and the main control center located there. "Marc's wife left him," Tris reminded.

Dominique's eyebrows rose. "Ooh. *La petite fleur* is having quite an effect on you, darling. Two weeks ago you wanted to strangle Marc yourself, and now you sound almost…ah, *sympathique?* Marc should have known better than to get married and not leave the agency. We all end up divorced."

"Did you say something to upset Hope?"

"Non. We were shopping, I told you. Though she kept insisting on picking up those trinkets for her kids rather than finding some clothing for her that doesn't resemble a sack. She looks too young to be a mother, I think."

Tris wanted to shake her. He pushed her into the seat he'd just vacated. "Watch the monitors," he said tightly. "If I can trust you not to turn your back on them."

Dominique pouted. "Darling—"

"Shut up, Dom." He walked out on her, closing the security door that kept the existence of the control center from a chance discovery by any curious hotel staff. Dom was good at her job. The best. She had been able to ferret out details about her targets that had been invaluable to their successes. But the woman was as annoying as a splinter stuck under your thumbnail. He didn't know how Cole stood her. But then, Cole was in Connecticut, wasn't he? Putting plenty of distance, on a regular basis, between him and the woman who occasionally shared his bed, if not his life.

He went downstairs, stopping only long enough to speak with Henri, another H-W agent who also served as the hotel's concierge, before heading out onto the narrow, street. If Hope returned before Tris did, Henri would take care of her. The man was a pillar of reliability and discretion, which was why he was so suited to his cover. Only the H-W agents who used the hotel as a base knew the true purpose of the hotel. The guests who returned year after year—the wealthy, the famous, the privileged—gave their loyalty because the exclusive hotel offered the height of elegance, service and privacy. Which kept anyone from noticing the other activities that occasionally occurred within its historic walls. Activities spanning everything from being a safe house to an occasional prison to a crash zone for operatives going to and from their various gigs.

Tris quickly walked through the streets, searching every shop, every café, for a glimpse of his errant bride. He didn't think she'd have quite the nerve to try the metro. And she had no money that he knew of—he'd told Dom to make sure Hope got whatever she needed. But then, he'd have never thought she'd deliberately evade Dom, either.

Dammit. This was all his fault. The rumors. The wedding. The fact that Hope was all alone somewhere on the streets of Paris, probably chewing the hell out of her soft inner lip, and hanging on to her gold necklace like a lifeline.

He stopped on the corner, absently noticing the chatter and the clink of glasses from the people sitting at the little umbrella tables of yet another outdoor café.

When he found Hope and made sure she was okay, he was going to strangle Dom.

"No, please, Henri. There is no need to call my...Monsieur Clay. I'll just go on up to my, ah, room."

"Monsieur Clay was very clear. He insisted." Henri was inflexible as he picked up a sleek black phone and punched in numbers. "Perhaps *mademoiselle* would like to leave her packages with me and have some refreshment?"

Hope looked over at the elaborately engraved windows that separated the restaurant from the rest of the minuscule lobby. Henri was as excruciatingly polite and courteous as anyone she'd ever met. But she also knew that the man had no intention of letting her up to Tristan's floor until he'd phoned.

She sighed and left him with the boxes and bags she'd collected on her afternoon adventure. She'd occupied herself just fine once she'd gotten rid of Dominique, she reminded herself cheerfully, as she entered the restaurant. That woman had been patronizing to the point of rudeness, telling Hope point-blank that if she hoped to ever get Tristan "in her bed,'' she'd better lose the doe-eyed country-girl act.

While Dominique had been aimlessly browsing a narrow rack of touristy T-shirts, Hope hadn't felt the least bit guilty for stepping into a crowd of laughing students, following them out of the shop and down the street.

Once on her own, she'd bought gifts for Gram and Justine and Jolie and Drew. She'd found delightful souvenirs that she would give to her class when school started in the fall. And for herself, she'd found a selection of relatively inexpensive T-shirts, a few pairs of capri pants and some underthings. She only hoped it was enough to get her through until their trip was over, because the next time she went out, she wanted to see the sights that were to be had *outside* of the expensive shops.

Her feet ached and she felt like she was positively wilting from having walked for what seemed miles. But inside, oh inside, she was beaming. Not even the small table she was escorted to in an oppressive corner near the swinging door of the kitchen was enough to dim her enthusiasm.

She smoothed her finger over the useless purse, biting back a smile as she looked at the linen-covered table. But the credit card she'd carried inside had been far from useless. And shopping in Paris was like nothing else in this world. She couldn't wait to try the metro and—

''Where the hell have you been?''

She jumped and looked up at Tristan standing in front of her table, wearing an annoyed expression. ''Henri called you.''

"You've been gone hours."

"There was a lot to entertain me."

He wasn't amused. "Did you get lost?"

"No!"

"Then where have you been?"

"Shopping. Wasn't that what you wanted me to do? Stay busy and out of your hair while you worked?"

He stared at her as if he didn't recognize her, then wedged his tall body into the other seat at the table. "You had no money," he gritted. "You didn't even have the telephone number here in case something happened."

She flipped open her purse and pulled out her credit card. "Plastic," she said flippantly. "Good all around the world, and I didn't even have to know the exchange rate. And I left a trail of bread crumbs so I could find my way home."

"Nice, Hope. Joke. In the meantime, I've spent most of the afternoon looking for you, instead of getting the work done that I've come here to do."

She hated the wave of guilt that swamped her at that. "No one asked you to go hunting for me as if I were a lost infant." She nudged up her glasses and smiled calmly. "As you can see, it wasn't necessary, because here I am. Safe and sound."

He sent away the approaching waiter with an impatient look. "What would you have had me do? Ignore your little disappearing act?"

"I'm surprised you noticed *what* I was doing while your friend is around tangling her long fingernails in your hair and calling you *darling*."

"Dom is an associate," he said impatiently.

Her tongue kept running away from her. "You sleep with all your female associates, then?"

His lips twisted. "Better them than the men."

"Oh!"

"This wasn't like you, Hope." He grabbed her hand and folded his fingers around it and just that easily the bubble of nerves and irritation and shaky confidence that had spurred her along all afternoon wobbled. Hard. "I can't help, if I don't know what's going on. Talk to me."

Hope tugged on her hand, and she folded it over the other hand in her lap. "I just would have appreciated it if you'd warned me what to expect when we arrived here."

"About what? The hotel? You knew I had to work."

"About…Dominique." She felt his narrowed gaze on her face and looked to the side at the other patrons. Couples mostly. Lovers. The whole city seemed to be filled with them. In the shops, at the cafés, on the sidewalks and in the streets. People strolling arm in arm, heads bowed together as if they shared some sweet secret known only to them. "It was a bit awkward, you know. I realize our, ah, marriage is purely for show, but it was still odd to be wearing your rings while you sent me off shopping with your lover."

"Lover?"

"I suppose I can understand why you didn't tell her we were married in Weaver. Might have cramped your style."

"Lover?"

"Why do you keep repeating it? Are you afraid

someone here in the restaurant didn't hear you the first time?''

"Sweet pea, Dominique is most definitely *not* my lover. And I think my boss Cole—the guy who is— might take exception to your insistence otherwise. I didn't tell them because it's none of their business. Marriages aren't real popular in my business, and I thought I was saving us both some grief.'' He leaned over the table, wrapping his hand behind her neck and inexorably tugging her close. "You're sounding remarkably jealous.''

She forgot her curiosity over what that "business'' was at that last remark. "I am not jealous.''

He ignored her protest. "Perhaps you *would* like our marriage to be a little less for show and a little more in deed?'' He didn't let go when Hope tried to turn away. "God knows you entice me. More than any female I can recall. I'd certainly like to get the kiss I wanted that got us into this mess. And I'd definitely find it no hardship to take you into my bed. But you'd be the one ending up on the short end of the deal, so consider yourself lucky that I have a few decent cells left in me.''

It was not the first time he'd said something like that. She remembered his caustic words on the flight—that he was all surface and no substance. She'd dismissed them at the time as another indication of the dry amusement that always seemed to hover beneath his surface. But now, with his lips a hair's breadth from hers and his strong fingers shaping the curve of her skull beneath her loose braid, she wasn't so sure. "Why would I be on the short end?'' she whispered.

His lids lowered, and she could *feel* the touch of his gaze on her lips. She thought her heart might well stop.

And then she didn't care, because he leaned that tiny bit farther and covered her mouth with his.

Hope had been kissed before. The first time when she'd been twelve and Jolie's brother had dared her into it one afternoon after school. But she'd eventually learned about the legacy left behind by her mother and by Justine, and Hope had kept her kisses to herself lest she bring any more embarrassment upon Gram. Until she'd gone off to college and met Johnny Mueller. He'd gotten past her defenses, all right. But even he hadn't made her tremble to her toes. He hadn't tasted of dreams—dark, dangerous dreams that sucked at her soul until she couldn't tell where she stopped and he began.

Tristan's fingers angled her head and she willingly went, forgetting that they were in that dark, overly warm back corner of the restaurant; forgetting that they were in a public place; forgetting that they were married only to put the gloss of respectability back on her name.

And when they finally broke apart, her breath tumbled past her lips and she swayed unsteadily. He rested his forehead against hers, sucking in a hard breath. "That's why," he said roughly. "I'd take everything you've got to give and it'd be a hell of a ride, but when we finally landed, you'd be left with nothing. You'd give me your heart. I can see it in your eyes."

Hope drew back and he let her. "Would that be

so bad?'' She smiled quickly, awkwardly, painfully. ''You said it yourself. We *are* married.''

He brushed his thumb over her lips and his lashes shaded his expression. A muscle ticked in his jaw. ''It wouldn't be bad for me. I'm the most selfish guy I know. I'd take it all. But I don't have anything to give back.''

She looked down at the table. He wasn't selfish at all. And despite Dominique's taunt earlier, Hope knew that Tristan possessed plenty of sentiment. ''Because I'm just a plain girl from Weaver and you're the golden-haired guy who keeps an entire Parisian hotel floor at his disposal.''

''No. Because you have a heart to give, Hope. And I don't.''

Chapter Nine

All told, they spent nine days in Paris. Hope learned to ignore Dominique's sharp humor on the few occasions they ran into one another, and to adjust to Tristan's undeniable capacity to focus himself. Since the…episode in the restaurant, Tristan hadn't given Hope one single glimpse of the man who had kissed her as if she was his salvation.

Of course, he was usually working at whatever it was he did in that room he'd thought she hadn't noticed; and when he wasn't working, he was preoccupied and tense. In fact, all of his associates, who came and went at all hours of the day, were tense.

But on one occasion when Hope had mustered some courage and broached the subject of Tristan's "business" with him, he'd shrugged and offered some pat explanation about computer programming that she hadn't believed for a moment. If it weren't for the fact that she knew just how deeply his honorable streak ran, she might be worried about what went on in that secret room. She wasn't worried, but she was curious. She had no intention of asking again, particularly since he'd made it plain that he wanted to keep the fact of their marriage separate from his work. If Hope wasn't going to go out of her mind, she had to get out of the hotel and away from those men and women who came and went, barely glancing her way as they went about their business.

With Henri's help and advice, and armed with a phrase book and guide to Paris, she'd discovered all the beauty and magnificence of the Louvre; lost her cheery beret to the gusting wind high atop the Eiffel Tower; and strolled along the Seine where artists painted and children played. She sat and had her portrait done in charcoal, because she couldn't resist the charming young artist who'd laughed her way. But she'd hidden the small canvas away in her suite because she didn't consider the rendition to look anything like her, and felt silly that she'd spent her money on something so frivolous.

She explored the garden outside the hotel, and lounged by the crystal-clear indoor pool. It was all beautiful and all wondrous but none of it matched the promise of spending a rare moment with the stranger who was her husband.

It wasn't wise to fall for him, she knew. He was confusing and difficult and had told her flat out that there was no future for them.

He hadn't kissed her again. But that didn't mean

she hadn't relived that moment over and over again. That she hadn't puzzled over his claim at being heartless. Goodness, a heartless man would have *left* her to face alone the rumors of their nonexistent torrid love affair. A heartless man wouldn't care about the schooling of the town's children. A heartless man wouldn't have requested the concierge of their hotel to see that every whim of Hope's was met.

That tidbit had obviously made the rounds beyond Henri, too, because Hope hadn't been seated at that dinky little table in the rear of the restaurant again. And to prove her own stupid sentimentality, Hope had wished she *had* been seated back there.

Then, just that morning, Hope had opened her bedroom door to Tristan's abrupt knock and he'd told her they were leaving the next day. Early.

She'd nodded and promised to be ready.

But, instead of turning on his heel and heading off to do whatever it was that put those new lines in his forehead and beside his mobile lips, he'd looked at her for a long moment, pushed a wad of French currency into her hands and told her to get a nice dress. Because they were going out that night.

So there she was. On the night of their ninth day in Paris, dressed in an outfit that the salesgirl in the exclusive shop had assured Hope was *très magnifique*.

With Tristan nowhere in sight.

When she'd thumped her knuckles on the seemingly solid wall that hid the secret room he disappeared into for hours on end, she'd gotten no answer.

Nobody came and went. Even Dominique hadn't been around with her acerbic humor.

Eight o'clock ticked past. Then nine. Finally, at half past, Hope gathered her purse and the light wrap that went with her little slip of a dress. If she stayed in the suite, she knew she'd drown in the despair that plucked at her with greedy fingers. She'd look in the mirror yet again, see the stranger staring back at her, and convince herself that no matter how much paint she used or what fancy dress she wore, she would never be a match for her gloriously handsome husband.

Husband. What an overstatement. He was the familiar stranger who had signed his name below hers on the marriage license he'd magically produced.

When she stepped out of the private elevator, the appreciative gleam in Henri's eyes went a small way to restoring Hope's flagging confidence. He kissed the back of her hand and gallantly escorted her into the restaurant. But Hope didn't think she could face sitting alone at one of the little round tables, so she went instead to the ornate bar and slipped onto a gilded seat. Henri ordered champagne for her despite her faint protest, told her again that she looked *très belle,* and returned to his post.

Hope warily wrapped her fingers around the glass that was set before her. She looked over her shoulder through the window at Henri. He smiled and tilted his head, obviously waiting for Hope to drink. She sighed and lifted it to her lips. The sparkling, golden liquid burst to life on her tongue and she closed her eyes.

Drinking champagne alone in a bar. Well, wouldn't Gram be proud of her now?

"I'm sorry I'm late."

Hope whirled. Tristan stood behind her, looking as spectacular as he had on their wedding day. Obviously it wasn't the tux that had taken her breath that day, because now he wore black trousers and a thin black sweater that clung to his broad shoulders. He was riveting.

Impossibly handsome or not, she had waited an hour and a half for him, she reminded herself, as she twirled the crystal between her fingers. She had spent all afternoon at a French-speaking hairdresser armed with nothing more than her phrase book and a terribly shaky determination to show Tristan that she could be...what? Like Dominique?

"The kiss of death," Tristan observed, watching her slowly sip.

It was the wrong choice of words. Hope couldn't prevent herself from looking at "their" little table in the back of the room. She set the glass on the bar and turned her back on it. She didn't want to be like Dominique. She wanted to be a normal woman, a kindergarten-through-third-grade teacher. She wanted the man she'd married to not look upon her as some needy little thing whom he had to protect.

"You look lovely," he murmured.

"Don't let the shock throw you."

He tilted his head, narrowed his eyes, and gave an exaggerated sniff.

"What are you doing?"

"Trying to figure out what is in the air that has affected you so."

She adjusted the filmy narrow scarf where it looped over her elbows. "I don't know what you mean."

That amused Tristan. "I don't know what you mean," he parroted. "Have you been taking lessons from Dom?"

"If you're going to be insulting, I'll go out by myself."

Tris eyed her, wondering when he'd blinked and his sexily shy sweet pea had been replaced by this sexily quick-tongued young woman. "You would, wouldn't you."

She nodded and slid off the stool. Tris nearly swallowed his tongue. He'd known she was curvy, of course. A man who enjoyed women as much as he did didn't reach his age without having some clue about what women could hide under baggy clothes. The dress she'd worn the day of the wedding had only hinted, and the thigh-length T-shirts and snug pants that stretched just past her knees that she'd taken to wearing over the last week hadn't been much better.

This dress—this confection of black silk that covered her from neck to knee—yet didn't—wasted no time at hinting. It announced. Loudly and boldly and tauntingly.

"Something wrong?"

She was pure woman from the top of her gleaming, toffee hair down to her toes, encased in high-heeled shoes that screamed sex. She was mesmerizing. And even more slender in the waist than she had been when they'd left Wyoming—and she'd been plenty perfect then.

He realized he didn't know exactly what she'd done during her days when he'd been tiptoeing through the bowels of Pirelli's computer systems, carefully planting the identities that would ensure the safety of his colleagues, and in turn, hundreds of others. "I'm hungry," he said truthfully.

Somehow she'd managed to make her violet eyes look even deeper and more entrancing—yet avoiding the overt look that women like Dom preferred, which also made him realize that she hadn't worn makeup at all before this. "You've done something with your eyes."

Her eyes flickered, but she didn't look away. "Is it just awful? Gram would say I was painting myself up like Justine if she saw me like this."

"Your Gram would say you looked like a beautiful woman," he countered. Ruby Leoni had obviously said a lot of things to her granddaughter. But one important truth she'd kept from Hope, and he didn't know if he agreed with her reasoning or not. But then he wasn't in any position to judge.

Hope was drawing the ends of the scarf through her fingers. "If you're hungry, perhaps we should eat," she said. "Or are we being joined by your associates?"

He shook his head, wondering if she was even aware of the motions of her hand on the scarf. Caressing.

He made himself think of the work—it was a hell of a lot easier on his nerves. The Pirelli case was coming along. His team had done its job, and now it was up to the guys in the field. Tris wouldn't likely be involved again unless there was a hitch in the extraction; otherwise, he'd be around for the debriefing when the dust settled and Pirelli was out of the illegal arms trade and on his way to an eternity in prison. Tris would make his final report, head back to his place in San Diego where he'd continue designing software for computer games until Cole contacted him with the details for their next op. Then he'd be on the move again.

It might take a week. It might take a few more. But Tris knew from experience that he wouldn't be at home for more than a month before something new came up. At least, that was what he'd done dozens of times over the last ten years. This time when Tris headed back to San Diego, he'd be taking along a passenger.

His wife. Yet not his wife.

A woman who tied him in knots simply with the way she absently toyed with that filmy black scarf.

"Tristan? Do you want to go, or not? Because I'm perfectly capable of occupying myself. There is a nightclub I passed the other day that I want to visit and—"

He slid his hand up her back and she went silent. "If you think I'm going to let you loose on the club scene here, you're dreaming."

"I'm of age and reasonably intelligent," she sputtered. "I've managed to keep myself safe over the past nine days."

"Thank God. But you're a walking invitation to men in that dress." He escorted her past Henri who smiled benevolently at them as the liveried doorman awaited their exit.

"I didn't buy this dress to gain attention from

strange men," Hope said. "I bought it to please myself."

"Does it?"

She glanced down at the dress. "I've never owned anything like it. Even Gram's dresses from when she was young don't compare to this. It's—"

"Almost worthy of the woman who fills it." He wrapped his arm around her shoulder, only, he reasoned, because they were crossing the uneven street and she wore heels that were so high he wondered how she could walk at all. She stiffened for a moment, then relaxed.

"It's so beautiful here," Hope sighed long moments later as they rounded a corner and the golden glitter of the Champs Élysées at night was laid out before them.

"It has its points," Tris murmured, watching the way the streetlights reflected on Hope's eyeglasses. "Nearsighted or farsighted?"

She glanced up at him, then away, and he realized that the veneer of confidence she'd acquired was not so thick, after all. "I need them for driving."

He stepped in front of her, uncaring that they were in the middle of the sidewalk, blocking the other people who were out strolling. "You're not driving now." She lifted one shoulder in a shrug, and the filmy wrap slid down her arm.

"So?"

"So," Tris yanked his gaze up from her shoulder, "let's try it without them." He slipped the gold frames off her nose and tucked them in his pocket before she could protest. "If you walk into the Seine accidentally, I'll let you have them back."

Her fingers lifted to her neck, and he knew that she wore her necklace under the black band of fabric that circled her throat. The dress started there, high on her neck and cut a sharp angle downward, covering everything except the whole of her shoulders and arms and a painfully tantalizing slice of flesh when she lifted her arm. It was simple and owed every bit of its appeal to the astonishingly perfect figure beneath.

"But I always wear my glasses," Hope protested faintly.

"Not tonight." He didn't want her hiding behind the protection of her eyeglasses.

"Afraid someone will see you with old four-eyes?"

Tris tucked her hand under his elbow and started slowly along the famous thoroughfare. "Nobody here knows me or cares about me." Certainly no reporters desperate for a story.

"Henri does. He says you don't eat enough when you're here. And Dominique."

"Henri is a fuss-pot, and we go way back. And Dom, well, who can explain Dom? She's brilliant and a pain in the neck."

"She's beautiful."

"If you care for the type," Tris agreed blandly. "Cole is welcome to her, I say."

They walked along in silence and with each step Tris tortured himself by focusing on the feel of her breast brushing against his arm.

"You were never involved with her, then? Ever?"

"I've kissed you more than I've kissed Dom," Tris murmured.

"But, you've...ah...kissed lots of women."

He looked down at her head. Her hair was twisted into an intricate knot on her head, but several long strands had worked loose. Or perhaps she'd left them dangling at her nape and her temple to drive him around the bend. "A few," he answered absently, not sure if she'd been making a statement or asking a question. "But I don't get involved with women—not the way you're implying." Not anymore.

"Ever?"

"I'm the computer guy, remember? So tell me, who was your first kiss?"

"Jolie's brother."

"You must've been pretty young. He died when he was fifteen or so, didn't he?"

Hope nodded. "He kissed me on a bet," she said after a moment. "To see if I was as...easy as Justine's legacy implied."

There was nothing but acceptance in her voice. No old anger, no hurt. Nothing. He pushed his free hand in his pocket. "Anyone since?"

She tilted her head and looked up at him sideways. "Other than you, you mean?"

He slowly grinned.

She rolled her eyes and slipped her hand from his arm, walking ahead. Tris watched her from behind, following along. He wondered if she had the slightest conception of how she'd blossomed here in Paris. He wondered if she knew that when she reached up to push a pin back into her hair, he could see the outer curve of her breast. Just the narrowest glimpse of velvety skin.

Mostly, he wondered why she hadn't answered him.

He caught up to her. "So was there anything in Paris that you wanted to see or do that you haven't?"

She shook her head, pushing in that pin yet again. "No. I'm sure Henri kept you well informed of my daily excursions."

Not enough to give Tris some advance warning of Hope's heart-stopping transformation. "Does that bother you?"

"Not as much as it bothered me to have you assign Dominique as my official keeper."

"I didn't do it to hurt you, Hope."

She nodded. "I know." She turned around and looked back up the avenue, ablaze in lights. "You were just doing what you do. Taking care of things. Protecting things."

"You're not a thing, Hope."

She looked down, and he followed her gaze. She was twisting the wedding set around her finger. "Sure I am. I was something else you were protecting. I suspect Henri thinks I'm just someone under your protection."

He frowned. The only protection she needed was *from* him. "I know you've called Ruby a few times. Everything okay back home?"

"Yes. Brenda's cousin-the-reporter came back and wanted to get interviews from the wedding guests, but Gram says everyone has closed ranks against that sort of thing. Even Bennett, oddly enough. Soon after, I guess, she was assigned to a food column. Now, everyone in Weaver is talking about how romantic it was, you sweeping me off my feet the way they think you did.'' She wouldn't look at him. ''Too bad they didn't do that before the wedding. You wouldn't be saddled with a wife you don't want.''

''I'm not saddled, Hope.''

Her lips moved, but her expression was too solemn for it to be a smile. ''Well. That's kind of you to say.''

And she didn't believe him for a second. He drew in a long breath. This was getting too deep. ''You had a club in mind?''

Hope nodded and pointed.

''All right then,'' he said smoothly. ''Let's get moving before I decide I'd rather stand here and keep you to myself.''

She shook her head, clearly disbelieving.

He could have convinced her easily enough. All he'd have to do would be to pull her into his arms, taste her lips again, and he knew they'd both forget the nightclub. They'd forget everything except each other.

But if he ever wanted to have a restful night's sleep again—something he figured *would* return in time if he didn't rock the boat too badly—he knew he couldn't go there. Not after that kiss they'd shared. The kiss, he was beginning to fear, that had been worth every minute of inconvenience and disruption it had caused—both before it had occurred, and after.

So it was definitely time to stop thinking about it,

he told himself roughly. He grabbed Hope's hand and strode toward the club.

It was crowded, but Tris was big and people just naturally stepped out of his way. He also knew the owner, so it wasn't long before he and Hope were inside where the music throbbed through their bones. There was every manner of dress inside and for a moment, Tris let himself see the place through Hope's wide eyes—bodies crushed together on the dance floor, cocktail waitresses wearing next to nothing serving everything from martinis to ginger ale.

Hope looked up at him, and he leaned down to hear. "Toto, I don't think we're in Kansas anymore."

But there was only sparkle in her eyes and Tris smiled. She was still the same woman he'd pushed on a swing one Sunday afternoon. There wasn't one logical reason they should have much in common, but he liked her. When he wasn't silently cursing them both for the want that ate at him from the inside out, that was. "Want to dance, or eat?"

She slipped the wrap off her arms and left it on the high stool she'd been using. Looping her fingers through his, she tugged him toward the dance floor. Her eyes flashed when she looked at him over her shoulder. "I want it all," she laughed. "Every last little thing!"

The fire in his blood leaped through every single pore. How in the hell was he supposed to resist her like this? It was hard enough when she had her schoolteacher persona firmly in place. Hard. There was a laugh.

Thank God the music was loud and fast. It meant he could keep the space of an inch or two between them. Because holding her against him right now would be an education for them both.

He couldn't remember the last time he'd gone clubbing. Probably not since Serena. She'd loved the nightlife in California. She'd said she'd loved him, too. But his dysfunctional heart had been untouched. Just as it had been when, a few months later, she'd left.

He wasn't human, she'd accused at the end. Her reasons were valid, the most valid in the world, he knew. She'd been deeply hurt and he hadn't been able to lie and tell her she was wrong about him.

In the minuscule, shifting bit of floor Hope had found among the revelers, she lifted her hands above her head, whirled to the music and showed Tris that when it came to his violet-eyed temptress, his humanity didn't count.

He was just a man who wanted to capture that whirling dervish and swallow her smiles and taste the skin that warmed her necklace underneath that drive-him-mad dress.

She suddenly danced close, and even among the throng he could smell the subtle scent of her skin; feel the warmth of her flesh; taste in his mind the bead of moisture that had formed at her temple. "What do *you* want?" she asked breathlessly.

"I want it all," he said, settling his hands on her shoulders, feeling the scorch of her bare skin against his palms. All his good intentions at that moment mattered not at all. He was just a man. And she, right or wrong, was his wife. "Every last inch of you."

Her lips parted. He groaned. And took them.

Chapter Ten

Over the edge of his laptop, Tris glanced at Hope.
Again. She was still peering out the window, and he
wondered what was so fascinating about watching
the wings of the jet cut through the layers of cloud.
Or, maybe she just couldn't stand to look at him.

He'd lay bets on the latter.

When he should have been finalizing his report
for Cole, he continued watching Hope's profile. The
smooth, clear forehead. The nose that was cut just
a little short at the end, saving it from an aristocratic
elegance and giving it more personality. Smooth,
rounded jaw with just a hint of stubbornness—the
grit she displayed more easily since he'd virtually
left her to sink or swim in Paris.

He should have known she and Dom wouldn't

become bosom buddies. Dom didn't exactly relate well with other women.

Well, Hope hadn't sunk. Not that he'd expected her to. She'd swam, she'd burst from the water in a miraculous spray of water. She'd blossomed. She'd soared.

"Think you'll miss Paris?"

Hope looked over at him, surprised. And why not? He'd barely spoken to her since they had left the hotel. Hours ago. They'd boarded the plane, and Tris had immediately buried his nose in work.

"It was unforgettable," she answered after a moment. Her attention turned again toward the window. "Almost like a *real* honeymoon," she murmured. "Except nobody but you and I knew we'd even exchanged vows."

Score for the lady.

It had been approaching dawn when Tris finally flagged down a taxi to take them back to the hotel. It wouldn't have taken a lot of effort on his part to gain an invite into her bedroom once they'd arrived. She'd had champagne again, she'd been bubbling with energy after their evening, and she'd been so tempting he'd had to nearly chew off his own tongue to keep from pursuing her.

He'd seen the confusion clouding her eyes when he'd kissed her chastely on the forehead and nudged her into her bedroom. Alone.

"I like home better." Hope's voice drifted slightly above the hum of the jet engines and he had to strain to hear.

"Weaver?"

She nodded. She rested her chin on her arm.

"Have you been to California?"

"No."

"Ever wanted to go?"

"Doesn't matter, does it? I'm going."

"Well, hell, Hope. All this enthusiasm of yours might just knock the plane off course. Be careful, would you?"

She looked at him again. "Why don't you like Weaver?"

"Who said I don't?"

"You rarely visit. It looked to me like you got on with your family just fine. What other reason is there?"

His thumb tapped his keyboard. "I don't dislike Weaver."

"Then it must be your family. Your dad, maybe? Because he married again? I know that bothered you."

"No," he said with exaggerated patience, "it didn't bother me. I'm not into weddings. Most men aren't, you know. My family is fine. They've got great lives. But that's their lives. Not mine."

"Married and starting families, you mean."

He watched her. "Why are you going on about this?" There was a small vein pulsing in her milky-pale temple.

"Remember last night when we were walking? Before we went to the nightclub?"

"It was less than eighteen hours ago, sweet pea. I remember."

"We were talking about you protecting everyone."

"Well, not exactly."

"Yes, exactly." She moistened her lips but didn't look at him. "I don't know at all what kind of work you were doing in Paris. But everyone deferred to you, you know."

"I'm not the boss. Cole is."

"Maybe so, but he wasn't there, was he? Everyone from Dominique to Henri to the garçon in the restaurant to the men who escorted us to and from this plane—they all looked to you for direction before making a single move."

If Cole had his way, Tris would eventually take over Cole's job as head of Hollins-Winword. Tris was even beginning to consider it himself. Mostly for the challenge. As usual, his interest in a job only went so far before he needed new ground. And it wasn't as if he had a personal life he'd be sacrificing for that life. "What's your point? You want me to give you the rundown on how I make my living?"

She moistened her lips, swung her knees around on the couch-style seat and wrapped her arms around them. "No. If you wanted me to know, you'd tell me."

"What if I was some kind of, I don't know, international jewel thief or something?"

"Oh, please. You'd never do anything...nefarious."

So she didn't know him so well, after all. "When I was twenty-three, I shut down NORAD's power grid. Hacked into the National Security Agency. Rerouted a couple of planes. Airforce One among them."

Her eyes blinked. Shock visibly rippled through her. "Oh my."

"It was either go to work for them or…"

"Or?"

"…or go to jail," he said flatly. What the hell was he doing? He didn't talk about his work. Not even Jefferson, who had been on the H-W payroll as a field agent for years, had known until just a few years ago that Tristan was even *part* of H-W, much less why. God knows he'd never felt inclined to admit getting nailed by the Feds eleven years ago. But if he hadn't been caught, Tristan's particular skills wouldn't have been made known to Coleman Black. Cole wouldn't have then negotiated for Tristan's services from the government, and God only knows what he'd have been doing since then. Punching out license plates, probably.

"Why did you do it? And what about your company? T-Comp, wasn't it?" Her voice was faint.

"I did it because I could," he said. "And my business was real. It made me a passel of money, particularly when I sold it." He'd made so much he'd never need to work another day in his life. But where was the fun in that?

"So you work for the government now? Is that why you're so secretive?"

"Not exactly."

Her soft lips compressed. "*Not exactly* seems to be one of your favorite phrases. And you're changing the subject again. You do that a lot when you don't want to answer something personal."

"It's not personal to tell you about my hacker days?"

She lifted her shoulder in a decidedly Parisian way. "You're legal now, right?"

"I'm not in danger of going to jail."

"Why doesn't anyone know about this? My life is an open book in Weaver—even if some of the people write their own passages on my pages. I've never heard *anything* about you like this."

"No reason you would. My work is confidential in nature."

Her eyes studied him and he felt a ridiculous urge to squirm in his seat. "You're protecting people," she murmured after a moment.

He shook his head, looking again at the open computer on his lap. "Don't start weaving fantasies about it," he advised. "It's not that interesting."

"Does your family know?"

"That I'm not that interesting? You bet."

"Do they know you keep those rooms in Paris?"

"They know I travel a lot."

"But not why."

She couldn't possibly know what a distraction she was, he thought. Not just her conversation, but her entire being. He'd been a knot of need ever since the nightclub. Hell, since well before that. Since a hometown café. "Does it matter?" he finally countered.

Her eyes narrowed and she ran the tip of her tongue thoughtfully along the edge of her pearly teeth. Her hair was pinned up with some sort of clip, and she wore a baggy white T-shirt with a picture of the Eiffel Tower running up the center. Snug, bright-red pants hugged her legs, ending just below her knees. She looked like a kid. And he wanted this version of her just as badly as he wanted the woman he'd left outside her bedroom door.

"Yes," she said after a moment, "it does matter."

"My brothers are aware of the general thrust of my work," he finally answered. "But we don't usually sit around yakkin' about it."

"The general thrust being *protection.*"

Thrust. Hell of a word to choose. He was slipping. His eyes lingered on her legs. "If you like."

"Which brings me back to my point." She moved her palm over her ankle. "Who protects you?"

He lifted his eyebrows. "Am I in danger?"

She grimaced. "Maybe from the people who sneak in and out of that secret room of yours in Paris."

Tris held back an oath. He'd known the likelihood of keeping Hope totally in the dark about the control center had been slim. He'd just hoped that she'd be preoccupied enough with exploring the city that she'd pay no mind to what else went on in the hotel. Shows how much he underestimated his wife. Under that good-girl, virginal exterior lay a mind that was plenty sharp. "They're my associates. I'm not in danger."

Despite the work he did for Hollins-Winword, it was the people who depended on his expertise who regularly walked their lives down the center divide of jeopardy's road. He tiptoed through cyberspace; peeking here, planting there. Creating identities, removing all traces of others. Rerouting, reconnoitering, reinventing. He did it to protect people like his brothers, Jefferson and Daniel and even Sawyer, to some extent—who'd spent years scattered out there trying to bring justice to a world where justice was a scarce commodity. Tris wasn't a dangerous guy. But he *was* single-minded. And the second time he'd gotten into the NSA system, he hadn't been caught. So he'd introduced them to a whole new set of system safeguards.

"That's not what I meant, anyway," Hope dismissed.

"I'm not sure I want to *know* what you meant," he murmured dryly. Truthfully.

She rubbed her hand up and down her bare calf. "I don't want you to share details of your work with me unless you *want* to. What I meant was who do you go to when you need protection?" She made an impatient sound and rose, pacing back and forth in front of him. "Who guards your heart, Tristan? Your fears?"

He was silent for a moment. "I told you already that my heart doesn't function that way," he said flatly. "And if I have any fears, it's more in the area of knowing we're alone on this plane except for the crew up there in the cockpit and there is a king-sized bed in that bedroom behind you just waiting to be messed up."

She stopped dead in her tracks. He hadn't returned her glasses to her yet, and he watched her eyes widen and look away. "There was a nice-sized bed in my room last night at the hotel, too," she said huskily. She looked at him again, a little frown pulling at her eyebrows. "I think you say things like that just to shut me up."

He smiled slowly.

"And you smile that way—all wicked-like—because you think it'll scare me off."

He dumped the computer on the table beside him. "If you're smart, it would."

"Don't you let anyone get close to you, Tristan?"

"Sure." He raised one eyebrow. "You want to come over here and sit on my lap? I won't object."

"You are impossible."

"And you are every inch a woman with all the needs to apply nicer labels on what is, essentially, a basic thing." Impatience ran through him. "Men want sex. Women want love. And they'll turn and twist it every which way from Sunday in order to convince themselves that sex *is* love."

"Who was it that twisted it on you?" Her eyes were flower soft.

"Nobody."

"Your brothers love their wives. Your father loves Gloria."

"I never said they didn't."

"So it isn't as if you don't believe in love. You just don't believe in it for you. That's so typical."

Tris smiled faintly. "I believe I'm being insulted."

"Maybe you are."

"And this, after I've sacrificed my sacred bachelorhood for you."

"No one asked you to," she said seriously. "You cared about the school, too. But you'll have it back—your sacred bachelorhood, I mean—soon enough."

The school was the farthest thing from his mind just then. "Why is that?"

"Because we're going to get an annulment."

"I've already told you that's not going to happen."

She propped her hands on her hips. "There are two of us involved here, you know."

"An annulment should occur only when a marriage hasn't been consummated."

Her cheeks went pink. "Well, there you go. No problem there."

He slowly pushed out of his chair. "You really don't believe that I want to take you to bed."

Now, her cheeks were red. Her soft lips compressed. "No," she blurted. "No man ever has."

"Who was the idiot who convinced you of that?" She didn't answer and he felt murderous. "Did you love him?"

"Did you love *her?*" she countered, her eyes pained. "The woman who twisted sex and love on you?"

The silence stretched between them. "You *wanted* me to follow you into your room last night," he finally said.

"I—Yes," she admitted, casting him a defiant look.

He'd never understand women. They were the most confounded creatures ever put on Earth. "If you want to have sex, just say so, Hope. Convince me that you understand that's all it can be, and I'm game."

She exhaled noisily. But her cheeks were nearly as red as those snug little half-pants she wore.

He pushed to his feet and grabbed her hand, pulling her toward the bedroom.

She gasped and dug her bare feet into the carpet.

He hid a smile and looked back at her. "Changed your mind so soon?"

Her chin angled and her eyes snapped. "Aren't you afraid I'll be so overcome that I'll burden you with my profession of undying love?"

"You'll be overcome all right," he murmured. Any minute now she'd tell him to take a flying leap. As well she should. His behavior was abominable.

But he had to get her to stop thinking about making love. He was thinking about it enough for *both* of them. His good intentions only went so far and right now, they were miserably thin.

It was his own fault. He should have continued keeping her at a safe distance instead of recklessly suggesting last night's "on the town" activities.

She toyed with her necklace. "Is this your plane or does it belong to the people you work for? The 'not exactly' government."

Where was she going with that mind of hers now? "Mine."

"Do you usually travel with women?"

"Hordes," he smoothly lied. "I have a regular flying orgy going on up here."

"I don't believe you. I think you haven't been close to a woman in years," she countered. "If ever at all."

It was a few bytes too close to the truth. He wondered warily why it was that Hope was the one who saw it. Not his associates, not his brothers, not even Emily. Only this girl-woman who had apparently dived impetuously into the woman side of that equation while wandering the streets of Paris.

He deliberately drew his finger along the fine line

of Hope's jaw. "I'm not out of practice, if that worries you. But if you've changed your mind about pursuing this, say the word."

She was blushing from her forehead to her toes. "Not at all," she assured him. Her chin tilted, challenging.

A war of wills, he thought, intrigued more than he wanted to admit. "Did you ever play 'chicken' when you were younger?"

He could see her mind busily processing. "I had more sense," she said, her tone lofty. "Are you suggesting that I have less nerve than you?"

"I'm sure of it, sweet pea. You're the one who has never done this before. Right?"

Her soft lashes narrowed, leaving a slice of violet gleam that, if he'd been a fearful man, would have made him distinctly uneasy. She moistened her lips and stepped closer to him. So close that her soft curves grazed against his chest. He could feel the warm rise and fall of every torturously slow breath she drew.

"Right," she murmured silkily. Her head tilted slightly. "Are you too warm?" She reached up and drew her fingertip across his forehead, feathering the hair at his temple. "You feel—" she sighed, and he felt the punch of it to his gut "—feverish."

He caught her hand. The steady, dull roar of the plane engines hummed around them, enclosing them in their own private world. He stared at her and she stared back. He knew she was as acutely aware of their absolute privacy as he. "This isn't a game," he warned. "It's not swings in the park. It's not champagne in Paris, and my control is in short supply. I know what I want, Hope. Are you sure you know what *you* want?''

Yes. Your heart. Hope looked up at his fingers, manacled so impossibly gently, around her wrist. She'd been half in love with him even before the day she spilled coffee on him in the café. He'd been the hometown boy who'd had the world by the tail. He'd been the stuff of girlish fantasies, the white knight who rescued the damsel in distress.

But who was the real Tristan Clay? The man who wore a tuxedo as if born in one, who'd spoken fluent French in the nightclub the night before? Or this man who wore faded jeans, athletic shoes with a hole building above his toe and a yellow-and-purple tropical print shirt that was saved from garishness only because it was so faded?

Either way, he'd been the man who had pushed her on the swing in the park. Who had surprised her with Chinese food and played video games with a five-year-old boy. But he was so much more.

She could see it in the lines fanning out at the corners of his sapphire eyes. Eyes that held so much of the feelings that he claimed his heart didn't recognize. A heart that protected others, but refused protection for itself. He was a mystery to her, yet she felt like she knew him better than she knew herself.

She looked down to see his free hand curled into a fist at his side. She reached for it, slowly sliding her fingers around his wrist, in the same way he held her. She didn't know if it was his pulse she felt against her thumb or her own.

Or maybe their hearts were both pulsing slowly, heavily, one in tempo with the other.

She swallowed, not with nervousness but with the sureness of putting her trust in a man whose entire being was focused on caring for those around him. Even if he couldn't admit it.

She met his gaze, feeling the warmth of that intense blue deep down inside where she trembled and ached for something she'd never known. "I want the same thing you want," she said, and her voice shook only a little. "Right here. Right now."

Her chest felt tight, her skin burning beneath her clothing. She could barely breathe, waiting. Waiting, while he looked at her, his eyes full of something she couldn't put a name to no matter how hard she tried.

And when he did move, it was almost in slow motion, his eyes flickering over the fingers that she couldn't wrap all the way around his larger, masculine wrist. But the slowness was deceptive and in less than a blink, he'd reversed the positions until he held that wrist, too.

She flexed her fingers, her hands held aloft—away from him, away from her.

"Why?"

One simple word. One complex question. She searched for words, but none came. "I—"

He exhaled a sharp breath and tugged her wrists, pulling her hard and tight against him. "Never mind," he growled. "I don't care."

Her head fell back under the onslaught of his lips against hers. She could feel every imprint of his long fingers as he spread them around her waist, up her back. Then she gasped, breathing his breath, when he lifted her right off her feet.

"Hold on." His lips moved against hers and she wrapped her arms around his neck. "I won't drop you."

"I know." She'd never felt more secure in her life. More alive. More sure. She felt his hand on her hip, on her knee, pulling her thighs alongside his strong hips. She tore her lips from his, pressing her forehead to his shoulder. Then he was moving, and she closed her eyes tightly. Oh, please, if this was a dream, let her never awaken.

The soft click of the bedroom door closing was not a dream. The give of the mattress under her bare feet was not a dream when he settled her there, standing, looking down at him.

She moistened her lips, pressing her hands against his shoulders, adjusting to the reversal of heights. Weak sunlight shone through the porthole windows on the other side of the bed, enough to make strands of his burnished hair gleam like it had been dipped in liquid gold. The glisten drew her trembling fingers like a magnet, and his hair felt cool and heavy and slick as satin.

He stood there, a muscle ticking unevenly in his jaw and let her fingertips explore. The shape of his head. The curve of his ears. The bridge of his sharp blade of a nose. The mobile curve of his lips.

Oh, his lips.

His lashes lowered and she felt his hands on the hem of her oversized T-shirt. Then he was drawing it upward. She tilted her head, moved her arms and the soft, warm cotton fell to the floor.

She could hear him breathing. Felt his eyes like a physical caress on her breasts that, until this exact moment, she'd always cursed. His hand smoothed up her bare arm, shaped her shoulder, followed the edge of white satin, the necklace that dipped into the valley between her breasts. Her mouth went dry, and her eyes felt heavy.

His palm slipped over one aching peak, so lightly she might have imagined it. ''Please,'' the word sounded on her lips without volition. Her fingers curled against his shoulder, grasping the washed-soft fabric. She didn't know for what she begged, only knew that his hands came up along her hips, tightening, soothing, tormenting.

His gilded head moved, and his lips touched her collarbone. Tasted her shoulder. Breathed against her breasts, warmed her skin through the thin fabric that separated them. Hope's knees went to water. ''Tristan—''

''Sshh. It'll be all right.''

She sank her teeth into her lip, sucking in her breath when he flicked the center clasp undone and peeled back the bra.

''Perfect.'' He flattened his palm against her spine and drew her toward him. Her flesh sang, bloomed, swelled. Felt perfect, only because of his kiss so reverent, the tip of his tongue so sinful. Hope pressed her cheek to his hair, gasping for breath. Her head spun with madness.

Then he was pulling back, leaving her swaying. But only for a moment—a moment when he yanked at his shirt and sent it flying. Then he was lifting her from the mattress, holding her against him, her breasts grazing his hard, sinewy muscles as he slowly lowered her feet to the carpet.

She was weak. Her grasping hands reached for purchase, found his belt loops, felt the sharp intake of breath he gave when her hands brushed against him. He suddenly covered her fingers with his hand, stilling her trembling.

"If you wanna stop, say so now," he gritted. "After this, you're mine."

Hope's lips parted. She struggled for speech. But words wouldn't come. She drew her fingertip over his ridged abdomen. Felt his muscles leap. She leaned forward, pressing her mouth against his chest.

He sighed deeply, and folded her against his chest. The contact made her head reel, her flesh seeming to soften and mold to his harder angles. She felt his hands on her hair, releasing the clip and her hair tumbled down her back, over his hands, around them. A moan rose in her throat when he threaded his fingers through the long strands, slowly wrapping his fists in it.

She wasn't sure who was trapped. Her or him. She wasn't sure it even mattered.

Instincts were all she had, and she reached for the metal button at the waist of his jeans. He went still and she looked up, seeing the grimace on his face. Uncertainty accosted her. He smiled faintly, but it wasn't with amusement. His eyes were dark, intense. He released her hair, and it slid over her shoulders, her breasts. "Keep going."

Her lips were dry. She swallowed and he made a soft sound, tilting her chin up with his thumb. His lips traced hers, his tongue teased. Her head fell back under the pressure, and the uncertainty faded as if it never was. She tugged at his jeans, and the button popped loose. It sounded as loud as a cannon in the stillness, and she couldn't help jumping.

He smiled faintly against her lips, and it was like sending champagne bubbles straight to her bloodstream. A breathless laugh rose in her throat and she pressed her palms flat against his abdomen, running them with ever increasing delight up his torso, exploring every ridge, every broad plane. His flat nipples tightened against her palms and she murmured in amazement.

"You're gonna be the death of me," he muttered with half a laugh. With one hand he yanked back the bedding and tumbled her onto the mattress. She saw him reach out, without looking, and rummage in the drawer of the nightstand. Hope's smile faltered at the evidence of his preparedness. But then he was kissing her again, her breath becoming his and his becoming hers and she forgot to care. Their clothes disappeared as if by magic.

His long legs slid along hers, his hands tormented, soothed and tormented again. She was surrounded by him, by his heat, his scent, his touch. And still, every nerve inside her screamed for more. His back was hot and flexed under her searching fingers, his shoulders were wide and roped with muscle. And there, oh, there, she could feel him against her.

And just when she didn't think she could possibly live another moment without *something,* he stopped. A sob burst past her lips. "Please—"

He pushed up on his arms, his head bent over hers. "I don't want to hurt you."

"You won't." Tears collected in the corners of her eyes. Oh, she loved him.

He growled something under his breath and pressed.

Her lips parted. He stopped. She arched against him, mindless with need.

His back bowed and he lifted her against him, swallowing her involuntary cry with his kiss. She didn't know where she left off and he began. Her senses fragmented, stunning her. She cried out his name.

Tris groaned, feeling her come apart in his arms, convulse against him. She was silken and hot and she was tight and every curve fit him like never before. She was living hope, and he couldn't stop, couldn't wait to make sure she was all right, couldn't do anything but take everything she gave and gave.

He pressed his face into her toffee hair and gave up the notion that he'd ever been in control around her. Then she pushed her fingers through his hair and pressed her mouth to his, shaking, arching. Breathless sounds of need in her throat, and still she gave.

Her name screamed through his brain.

And he was lost.

Chapter Eleven

"I've never brought a woman on this plane," Tris admitted against her ear a long while later. His fingertips slowly trailed along her spine, content for the moment to indolently caress each little ridge under her satin-smooth skin. "Only you."

She was draped over his chest, her body sweet and warm and lax. "Your well-stocked drawer suggests otherwise," she murmured.

"Cole's sense of humor," he admitted blandly. "Been there, unused for a long while. Let's hope there's not an expiration date or something."

Her eyes drifted shut. "Thank you," she murmured sleepily.

"For what?"

"Making me your wife," she whispered.

Tris didn't answer. But she didn't notice, because she'd fallen asleep.

He stared into the shifting shadows of his airborne bedroom, absorbing the warm weight of her snuggled against him; absorbing the clean scent of her hair that spread over them both as she slept.

She was his wife. It was true.

Making love to her was like nothing he'd ever experienced, and the knot inside his gut told him that it wasn't because he'd been alone for years.

It was because she was Hope.

Kindergarten-through-third grade teacher.

Who saw enough to ask stinging questions about protecting his heart.

He could make love to her for the next millennium and never tire of her. He knew it with everything inside him.

But that didn't mean he had the heart to love her.

Against him, she made a soft sound. Satisfied. Sexy.

He closed his eyes and gently nudged her onto the bed beside him. It was better to leave now, than lay there with her, waiting for the inevitable urge he would get to escape. It would come. It always did, but he'd never before dreaded it.

He'd do exactly what he'd warned her of that first day in Paris. He'd take everything she had to give, and in the end she'd have nothing.

God help him, he didn't know what he could do to change it. He was a pathetic excuse of a man that he would take what physical pleasures she offered, knowing he was incapable of giving back the emotion she deserved. He'd married her to save her from one hurt, only to risk her heart in another way.

She sighed again, her hand sweeping along his hip, staying him when he would have left the bed. "Don't go," she mumbled, her hand gliding over his chest to settle over the spot where his heart beat. "I'll protect you," she murmured.

Tris went still. He looked down to find her violet eyes watching him. Her fingertips felt like burning pokers against his chest, and his heart, that unfeeling organ, jerked like an engine about to fire.

Time seemed to stand still as he waited—waited to see if he felt something there; something that would tell him he wasn't the inhuman freak he'd been accused once too often of being.

He felt Hope's gaze and the urge to get out of there, now, right this second now, slammed into him. And it wasn't anything like the "morning after jitters" he'd detested so much that he'd simply stopped getting involved with women that way. This was pure hell and just getting out of the bed wasn't anywhere near enough distance to put between them.

But where could he go? He left jumping out of planes to thrill-junkies like Jefferson.

Her lashes lowered over her eyes and he saw the long, smooth line of her throat move when she swallowed. She shifted on the bed and the tangled sheet didn't quite follow, barely sliding over one creamy hip.

Tris sat up, fierce want tangling with that mighty urge to escape. He knew he should look away, that his frank regard of her was probably unsettling her, despite what had just occurred. But he couldn't.

Innocence still shone from her face, but her beautiful, full breasts were peaked, wantonly inviting. Then she slowly drew up her left leg, her knee bending; slender, arched foot gliding on the mattress.

She could have been a model for an ageless painting—wanton innocence. The white sheet draped diagonally over her hip, revealing but not revealing. Her skin shone like a pearl, cool to the glance, but he knew if he touched her she'd be warm. As Tris watched, Hope touched the necklace.

But now, she didn't work the chain back and forth between her thumb and forefinger as she did when she was uncertain. She let the necklace lay, and watched him through her lashes as she slowly, so slowly, followed the gold links with her fingertip.

He wondered why the top of his scalp didn't explode from the blast of heat that rose in him.

She wasn't uncertain at all, he realized. She was seducing him with nothing more than the slow glide of her fingertip along a necklace that held—of all impossible things—a wedding ring.

"Why?" he asked.

Her soft lips curved faintly. Her fingertip reached the man-sized ring at the end of the necklace and began inching upward once again. He braced his hand on the mattress and decided abruptly that his efforts at keeping the sheet bunched at his own waist to protect her sensibilities was laughable. She was the one who was shocking him to his soul.

"You are my husband," she finally said.

"You knew I didn't intend for us to end up like

this when I proposed.'' His eyes roved over her re-
clining form.

"Because I was too young and too innocent for
someone like you."

"Because you believe in happily ever after."

"And you think you don't."

"Women want more than I have to give."

"*I* want more than you can give, you mean."

He knew it for a fact. "You deserve more."

She nibbled her lip for a moment, sending rockets
through his nerves that were already frayed and shot.
Then she lifted her hand, palm upward.

"I don't read palms."

She didn't smile. Her hand didn't drop. Just extended toward him. Vulnerable. Open. Accepting.
"You deserve more, too, Tristan," she said quietly.

Maybe he did. But he'd given up, years ago, expecting the same things out of life that other people
took for granted. He'd never quite felt like he operated on the same level as the world around him.
He saw problems, figured them out and corrected
them. He could practically read some people's
thoughts just from watching them from a distance.

But he'd never felt what they did. He'd tried.
God, he'd tried. There had even been a time when
he'd been with Serena twelve years ago that he'd
thought…perhaps.

Before marrying Jefferson, Emily had lived right
in his house for several years in California. She'd
been his best friend. She knew him about as well as
anyone could and even with her he had felt a chasm
between the emotion that could easily have been

there but wasn't. Which was just as well, since Em had been in love with Jefferson since she was a kid.

And still Hope's palm reached out toward him. Not grasping for him. Just waiting.

His chest felt tight. He looked out the porthole windows, saw nothing but the stream of white clouds. "I don't know how to love," he said abruptly. "I'll use up all of yours and leave you with nothing."

She blinked slowly. "Did it occur to you that I'm not offering you my love? That I haven't offered you the ring on my necklace?"

He looked at her, then. Brave words. Her violet eyes were practically swimming with emotion. He recognized love, even if he was incapable of feeling it himself.

And still her hand was there. To take, or not.

His wedding rings were on that hand even if he'd been unable to reciprocate by wearing a ring himself. He knew that there would never come a day that he wouldn't make certain that Hope was provided for. No matter what came later, she'd never be out of his life. Not completely. "I'm a wealthy man," he said.

A faint line appeared between her eyebrows. "So?"

"So you'll never want for anything. You can take Ruby sailing around the world if you choose. Move to San Francisco or Manhattan or Paris or Nantucket."

"Gram doesn't like boats since my grandfather died on one when they were still practically newlyweds, and I live in Weaver, which is exactly where

I want to live. Stop thinking you need to salve your conscience.''

"I'm not. You're my wife. You need to understand what that means. You'll inherit a sizeable estate someday."

"I didn't marry you for your money."

"I know that." He avoided her extended palm and reached for his jeans. He hitched them over his hips and moved across the bedroom to the intercom that connected to the cockpit. He buzzed, confirmed their flight status, and turned to look at Hope once more.

She'd sat up, and her hair flowed around her shoulders. Both her knees were drawn up under the sheet, and her hands were wrapped around them.

No longer extending toward him.

He told himself he was glad.

He *was* glad. It was better for her. Better for him.

"You married me because you were between a rock and a hard place with the school board," he said. "I put you in that place so it was only right that I get you out of it."

"Very accurately stated," she murmured. She pushed back the sheet and reached for her clothing. She dressed, not looking at him. "And I apparently married the pot of gold at the end of the rainbow, too. How nice."

He felt like scum. Not only because of his words, but because he didn't bother trying to turn his eyes from the sight of her. He couldn't have managed it had he tried.

She raked her hair back from her face and looked around. He handed her the clip. He wanted to tell her to leave it down. But knew he had no right to do so. "It's better that we keep things clear between us, Hope."

"I'm perfectly clear," she said calmly. "You're the one who is all muddled up inside, focusing on things that don't matter so you don't have to face the things that do." She stepped past him and pulled open the door. "I think I'll go sit up in the cockpit for a while. Will your crew mind very much?"

His jaw was tight. "No."

She smoothed her long shirt over her thighs. "You think I'm going up there to get away from you."

"Yes."

She shook her head, looking up at him with eyes whisper soft. "I'm going up there so *you* don't have to get away from me." She lifted her hand and he very nearly jerked when she touched her fingertips to his chest, right where his heart didn't beat with the emotions everyone else on earth seemed to have the ability to feel. "Do you still want to know why?"

She wasn't talking about the cockpit. She was talking about making love with him. About giving him her virginity. Her innocence. Her love.

"Yes." It was a bald-faced lie. He didn't want to hear what she had to say. He didn't want it on his conscience. Wasn't sure he could bear it.

She idly tapped her finger against his chest. She smiled softly. "Liar."

Then she turned on her bare heel and walked through the main cabin toward the front of the jet.

* * *

Their landing in San Diego was considerably different than when they'd arrived in Paris. There was no group of stone-faced men to greet them. No limousine. No floor of a hotel, no Henri.

Just a sizeable, graceful house that was what Hope figured must be the quintessential California dwelling. Tristan pointed to it when it came into view as they drove up a narrow, curving street.

The house sat well above street level and in the fading, gentle light of early evening, it looked entirely welcoming. A brick walkway and steps led up to an enormous black door in the center of the cream stucco structure. The roof was brick-red Mexican tile and the windows were arched. It was beautiful. And not at all what she'd have expected of Tristan, given the sketchy details she knew about his life. It was large and elegant, yes. But it was still in a neighborhood with other houses. It wasn't surrounded by fence or anything. It was, she thought with surprise, a regular house.

He thumbed a button, and the garage door opened. He drove the pickup that had been parked in a private lot at the airport right inside the garage. The door lowered behind them, momentarily throwing them into darkness. He shoved open his door and climbed out, hitting a switch on the wall that controlled an overhead light.

Hope swallowed and told herself to keep it together. The last thing Tristan needed was for her to be the weak-kneed Nelly he'd rescued by virtue of a wedding ring. She didn't know what demons dwelt inside him, but that they were present was not in question.

He'd made love to her as if they'd never have another day together on earth, and then he'd denied the emotions that she knew with every fiber of her soul he *did* feel. Just as she knew with every fiber of her soul that he wouldn't—couldn't—recognize it.

Maybe their marriage was a mistake. But Hope couldn't regret it. Not because of his wealth, or Paris or private jet. But because, when Tristan looked at her with his eyes ablaze with azure flame, she felt beautiful. She felt brave. She felt like a butterfly who'd been set free from a stifling cocoon.

The door beside her opened, and she looked up at him. She could see the shadows under his eyes and wondered when he'd last slept.

"Home sweet home," he murmured.

Hope slid off the seat and moved away from the truck while he retrieved his duffel and the suitcase Henri had produced for her to pack the purchases she'd made. She looked around the enormous garage.

Alongside the pickup were two motorcycles and on the other side of them was a sleek, wicked-looking convertible sports car. An expensive-looking racing bicycle, a surfboard and an assortment of other sporting goods were hanging from heavy-duty hooks. "Looks like a sporting goods store in here," she commented. He had every piece of equipment she could think of, but it all looked new. Unused.

He glanced around at the items, staring at them as if he'd never seen them. "Guess it does," he agreed blandly.

He shouldered the truck door closed and carried their bags around the truck and up three steps. There he punched in a code on a panel beside a door before opening it and waited for Hope to enter.

She stepped past him into a laundry room that was so typically familiar it made her immediately feel less like she'd tumbled down yet another rabbit hole.

He followed her into the room and she continued forward, entering a spacious kitchen. Well, it would have been spacious if not for the large electronic video game sitting between the table and a white-tiled breakfast counter.

On the table was a foot-high stack of hardback books, a computer printer and several other pieces of electronic equipment that she couldn't even hazard a guess at their purposes.

She eyed the mess. Did he ever stop working? Other than the days in Weaver before the wedding, and their last evening in Paris, he'd never once relaxed. Always with reports, paperwork, charts on which he scrawled indecipherable notes and symbols. She was fairly certain she'd seen him with at least three different laptop computers; one had looked similar to the one that the school had purchased last year for her classroom and one had been as slim as a narrow pad of paper. ''Cozy,'' she commented.

He grunted, dumping their bags onto the nearest surface, which happened to be the top of the video game. ''I wasn't expecting company,'' he said. ''I'll call the cleaning service in the morning.''

She folded her arms, looking around the kitchen. There was a dead fern sitting next to the stove. The phone on the wall rang stridently, startling her. But he ignored it and gestured for her to follow him.

They entered a high-ceilinged, tiled hall that separated the kitchen from a great room, beyond which she could see what looked like an atrium, complete with trees and pots of plants.

"Pool is through the jungle over there," he said. "My office is at the end of this hall. There's a bathroom down here and four upstairs, plus bedrooms. Take your pick. I've gotta make some calls, then I'll see about scrounging us up some food."

Hope nodded. His expression was already distracted as he headed for the office he'd spoken of. Obviously, he wasn't plagued with the vividness of their so-recent lovemaking the way she was whenever she looked at him.

Well, what did she expect from a man who had shut off his feelings?

She returned to the kitchen and opened the refrigerator door. Two long necks and a moldy block of cheese. She sighed and opened a few cupboard doors. She found cleaning supplies in the laundry room and set to work. Cleaning service. Hah. If she was going to be here for even a few days, she wasn't going to sit around by the swimming pool, twiddling her thumbs.

Two hours later, the kitchen sparkled. She couldn't do anything about the video game. She'd tried pushing it more to the side of the room, but it weighed a ton.

She'd carried her suitcases into the laundry room and started a load. But that didn't take long, which left her warily eyeing his leather duffel.

She finally decided she was being ridiculous, so she yanked open the zipper and pulled out a handful of shirts and jeans and plain old white B.V.D.'s.

She moistened her lips and hastily pushed it all in the washer. In the bottom of the duffel was a pad of paper and she pulled it out. Tristan's distinctive scrawl covered the page, but she couldn't begin to decipher the mathematical notations. She set it on the ironing board that she'd discovered was built into a nifty cupboard.

Tristan still hadn't emerged from his office and Hope dusted and mopped. Though the kitchen had been a jumble, the rest of the house was as neat as a pin. Barely used.

She carried their clean laundry upstairs, and decided that Tristan's room surely must be the large one with the wall of video tapes and big-screen television opposite an unmade king-size bed.

She found clean sheets in the hall closet and changed his bedding, smoothing the dark brown comforter up in place. And then, because she was tired, or because she just couldn't resist, she sat down, her hand absently stroking the bed beside her.

There were a few photographs in frames on the shelves among the videos, and impossibly curious about the man she'd married, she went over to look. One was of Emily Clay, wearing a graduation cap and gown. Another was an old black-and-white photo of Tristan's father and his first wife, Hope realized, looking with interest at the woman. Tristan had inherited Squire Clay's extraordinarily chiseled features, the hard, angled jaw and sharp blade of a nose. But Hope could see the resemblance to his mother, as well.

She nibbled her lip, slowly reaching for the frame. "You've been busy."

Hope jumped, shoving the picture frame back on the shelf. Then realized she'd tucked her hands behind her back like she'd been caught snooping. Which, of course, she had been. But it was only a photo.

"I put your clothes on your dresser there," she said, nodding at the neat stacks of T-shirts and socks and jeans. The Hawaiian prints and the plain-Joe briefs. She felt her cheeks heat.

He rubbed his jaw and Hope's fingers tingled as if she, herself, had brushed her hand over the golden-brown stubble shadowing his jaw. "You didn't need to clean," he said abruptly. "I didn't bring you here for that."

"I'm not exactly a guest, either," she pointed out.

He tilted his head in agreement. And Hope, once again, noticed the weariness in his face. In the too-controlled angle of his shoulders when he leaned his hip against the dresser.

"Where did you put your clothes?"

It was a simple enough question, but she felt, suddenly, as if she were treading in deep waters. "The room closest to the stairs," she said after a moment. She'd chosen it simply because of the lovely needlepoint pillows that were stacked on the bed.

"Emily's old room," he murmured.

Hope crossed her arms. Emily Clay was beautiful with deep brown hair that reached past her shoulders and eyes as expressive and brown as eyes could be.

And Hope knew that the other woman had lived here in this house for quite some time before marrying Jefferson several years earlier.

"We were friends," Tristan said quietly, as if he'd read her forming thoughts. "Still are. But that's all it ever was. She only had eyes for my brother."

"You didn't mind?"

His lips twisted. "I'm not tearing myself up with unrequited passion for Em," he assured her dryly.

The relief of that was enormous. Unexpectedly so, and it dislodged her tongue just as unexpectedly. "Then she wasn't the one who—" She broke off, feeling like an idiot.

"Who…what?"

Hope shook her head, waving a hand. "Nothing. Look, is there a grocery store in the area? My stomach is about as empty as it's ever been and I—"

"Hope."

"—could fix us something quick. You look like you could sleep a week and—"

He crossed the room without her having been aware of his moving. One moment he was over by the door, the next he was covering her lips with his. She caught her breath, reaching for his shoulders without volition.

When he lifted his head, she swayed unsteadily. "I've never driven a truck as big as yours, but I'm sure I could manage."

His eyes were amused and her words finally dried. "Sweet pea, after seeing you in action in Paris, I'm positive that you can manage anything you set your mind to. There's no doubt about it."

Her throat constricted. He meant it. Not just about

something as simple as procuring groceries or driving an unfamiliar vehicle. The backs of her eyes suddenly burned.

And it was as if a light snapped off inside him. The amusement disappeared as if it had never been. He let her go and turned away, lifting one hand to the back of his neck as if to squeeze away a pain. "I'll order Chinese," he said smoothly.

Hope didn't know whether to cry or hit him over the head with one of his laptop computers. There was one sitting right there on the shelf, within easy reach. "Chinese would be fine."

He was insistent that he didn't feel the emotions of an ordinary man. It was true—Tristan wasn't an ordinary man. He owned a jet, yet wore very pedestrian underwear. He doodled pages and pages of incomprehensible equations, yet owned an astoundingly extensive collection of Three Stooges videotapes. He made love but insisted it was only the meeting of two bodies.

He was a man of complete contradictions, and he had faith she could do whatever she set her mind to. And since that first real, unforgettable kiss they'd shared at that cramped little table in the hotel's restaurant in Paris, Hope now finally accepted that there was only one thing she wanted in life—capturing Tristan's heart as thoroughly as he'd captured hers.

She also knew the odds of that happening were on a par with the world turning flat.

Chapter Twelve

Tris hung up the phone and rubbed his eyes. God, he was beat. The Pirelli case was a wrap, all parties safe and accounted for. This was the time he was supposed to feel the high of accomplishment. The satisfaction of justice being served.

He didn't know what he felt.

A soft sound at the door to his office drew his attention. Hope stood there, a wooden tray in her hand.

He felt completely frustrated, he thought, with no small amount of unpleasant humor.

"I brought you some lunch," she said.

Over the past week, she'd taken to bringing him a meal in the middle of the day. Today was no exception. She'd deposit the food she prepared and leave him with a meal he ate out of necessity, and a desire he dared not quench. "You didn't have to."

"So you've already said," she countered. She walked across the room and set the tray on the side of his desk. Thick slices of homemade bread and chunky chili guaranteed to singe the taste buds off his tongue. Just the way he liked it. "I can't help it," she continued. "You stay holed up here in your office all day long. I feel guilty. I need to cook something to eat for myself, anyway. We can't eat out for every meal."

"Wanna bet?" Tris broke off a piece of bread. He knew for a fact that his kitchen didn't have a bread-making machine. Emily had had one, but she'd taken it with her when she'd gone back to Wyoming for good. Hope made this bread the old-fashioned way with her own hands. Mixing, kneading, shaping. He knew. He'd watched her when she hadn't been aware of it.

She rolled her eyes and tucked her hair behind her ear, heading once more for the doorway. "Well, I didn't mean to disturb your work."

Tris watched her, frowning suddenly. "You've cut your hair." It didn't reach the curve of her seductive rear anymore. It hung loose in a glossy thick curtain, but it only fell to the middle of her back.

She looked over her shoulder at him. "A few inches."

"What on earth for?"

"You were the one who arranged that personal shopper and the day at the spa. Obviously, you expected me to do something with my appearance."

"Your appearance was fine," he said impatiently.

"I just thought you'd enjoy it." Didn't all women like that primping sort of thing?

Her shoulder lifted and she smiled faintly. "I did." She waved her hands. "My nails are glossed, my face has been de-something or other, my body's been buffed and—"

Her words continued, but his brain took a short circuit when she mentioned buffing her body. He jabbed the spoon into his chili and thought about the least appealing thing he could. "There's another charity thing tonight."

"Oh. All right. You seem to get invited to a lot of these things. That dinner the other night. And the auction."

"I'm on a few boards," he muttered. "You don't have to go tonight. It'll be just more of the same. Too many people jammed into too small a place, too much noise, smoke, booze."

"I don't mind."

Of course she didn't mind. It didn't matter what curves he threw her way, Hope handled it all. Usually with a sweet smile and touch of pink in her cheeks that generally won over even the most jaded of his acquaintances. "Nah. I think we'll both skip it tonight," he said, wishing he hadn't brought it up in the first place. What the hell was wrong with him?

She returned to his desk. "What is it for?"

He watched her fingertip trace along the corner of the wood surface. "Chalmers House," he murmured. He'd been good. He hadn't touched her since that one kiss the day they'd arrived.

"You told me that was your favorite project," she

said. "It's a crisis center for abused women and children right?"

He nodded absently. He'd kept his hands to himself, and she'd kept her hands to herself.

It was killing him.

"You seem to support a lot of programs that help women and children."

"Tax deductions," he dismissed.

"Right. It's not a crime to want to help others, you know. You paid an astronomical amount for that painting at that charity auction the other day, because you knew the money would go toward such a good cause."

He'd bought the painting, donated by a local artist for the auction, benefiting a center for the homeless, because he'd seen the way Hope's attention had lingered on the wintry landscape. Because he'd liked her stunned surprise when he'd handed it to her. "Did you and that shopper lady find a swimsuit?"

She blinked. "Well, yes."

He pushed aside the food and stood. "Go put it on. I'll meet you out back."

"But I—" Her cheeks went pink. "All right."

He watched her go, a swish of long hair and cheery red shorts and shirt. Maybe submerged in the cold water of his tree-shaded pool he could get rid of the constant heat riding in his gut for her.

Hope's hands shook as she pulled on the one-piece bathing suit over which Julie, the "shopper-lady," had raved. Once she'd pulled the narrow straps over her shoulders, Hope looked at her reflection in the wide bathroom mirror and wasn't so sure.

For one thing, it was black. Not just black. It was shiny black. A shiny black that shrieked ''look at me.'' It was a one-piece, but the legs were cut so high on her hips that she felt more naked than not. The scoop top seemed too low, and Hope tugged and pulled as much as she could.

She'd bought the suit with some vague notion of lying out and getting a bit of a tan. Or rather, Tristan had bought it. He'd made the arrangements with the shopper for the clothing that now filled the closet and drawers upstairs in the bedroom Hope was using, and that had been that.

Hope started to pull her hair into a ponytail, but decided to leave it loose. If she pulled some of it in front of her shoulders, it helped cover some of that bare skin. She didn't need to add feeling naked to her unsettled stomach.

Aside from the few charity functions they'd been to, Tristan hadn't deliberately sought out Hope's company since they'd arrived. That he would do so now, today of all days, wasn't something she wanted to examine too closely.

She left her necklace on the dresser and, at the last minute, dragged one of the over-sized T-shirts she'd bought in Paris over her head.

Feeling better, Hope slid her feet back into her casual sandals and went downstairs. He was already in the pool, and Hope hauled in a shuddering breath as she walked out of the house.

His hair was darkened by water, making his sapphire eyes seem even more vivid. And those vivid eyes watched her steadily as she walked over to one of the cushioned lounges. Her knees felt shaky, and she gratefully sat on the edge of the lounge.

"Put on some sunblock," he said tersely. "Bottle is on the table there."

He disappeared beneath the surface of the glittering blue water, and she watched his water-wavery form travel the entire length of the pool without once coming up for air.

She absently reached for the bottle and applied some lotion to her legs. The bottle dropped from her slippery hands when Tristan surfaced by her toes, sending a cascade of water droplets over her feet.

"Ready?"

"Ah...I'll just lay here." She managed to smile even though she felt like a ninny.

He flattened his palms on the textured surface around the pool and pulled himself smoothly out of the water onto the edge. Hope's stomach clenched, and she blindly reached for the bottle she'd dropped. He was so bare. Too bare.

His wet hand closed around her ankle. "Come on in. Water's not too bad, today."

His thumb swirled over her instep. "I'm sure it's fine," she said breathlessly. "But, uh, I...don't... don't swim."

"Don't, or can't?"

His lashes were spiked together with water. She tore her gaze from his eyes only to have it land on that broad chest. That broad, bare, tawny chest. "Can't," she said, trying for another safe thing to look at. It wasn't his legs, dusted with hair and defined by long, roping muscles. She settled for the hand he'd flattened on the cement beside him. But even that was very near the dark blue swim trunks he wore.

"You don't know how to swim? Why didn't you say so earlier?"

The corner of his lips curved gently, and he pushed to his feet, pulling her up, too. "Come on." He headed toward the other end of the pool.

"Tristan, really, I don't care all that much about swimming."

He ignored her and stepped into the water where there were long, shallow steps leading down to the bottom. Hope hung back, but he held out his hand, palm up. "It'll be fine," he assured her. "This is the shallow end. Only three feet or so."

Shallow. Maybe the water was, but with Tristan she'd been out of her depth since the beginning. A knowledge that didn't stop her from putting her hand in his and stepping down onto the first step. He grinned and she took another step, just to see that smile again.

Before she knew it, her feet were on the bottom of the pool and the chilly water was lapping high around her waist, dragging heavily at the T-shirt.

"Let's get rid of this." Before she could protest, he tugged the shirt up and over her head, tossing it with a wet slap onto the side of the pool. Then his gaze drifted over her, and she thought she heard him mutter something under his breath. But he merely put his hands on her waist. "You're not afraid of the water?"

She shook her head, her thoughts numb.

He stepped further into the pool until it came up to Hope's chest. "Let your feet float up."

She swallowed. Tall trees surrounded the pool, and it suddenly seemed terribly private—utterly silent except for the rhythmic slap of the crystalline water. She lifted her feet, felt his arms slide under her and found herself floating on her back. "Oh!"

He smiled slowly.

She floated on her back. She floated on her stomach. He held her by the hands and towed her to the middle of the pool where even he couldn't reach the bottom, and she kicked and splashed. She watched the deep lines in his forehead ease.

And she fell in love with him all over again when he threw back his head and laughed.

When the phone rang a short while later, she swallowed a sigh and told herself not to be too greedy. He climbed from the pool and grabbed up the cordless unit that sat on the umbrella-covered glass table.

Tris couldn't take his eyes off Hope. She was standing in the shallow end near the side and as he watched, she bent her knees and tipped her head back into the water. Her hair floated around her in a glorious cloud.

The black swimsuit molded her in such perfection that his palms itched. Torture, insanity. Holding her in his arms, their water-slicked legs brushing against each other.

He wanted his wife.

But it wasn't fair to her. That *want* without love.

Swearing under his breath, he turned his back on the distracting sight and answered the phone.

* * *

"People who say women change their minds a lot haven't met you," Hope murmured. She was trying to fix the crooked black bow tie that circled Tristan's pristine white collar. But he kept fidgeting, reminding her strongly of one of her students who couldn't wait to go out for recess and play. "First you say you want to go to this thing tonight, then you say you don't. And now we're going again. If you don't like these benefit galas, why do you agree to go? You can donate your money and time without the parties, can't you?"

"It's expected," he said flatly. "You should know about expectations."

Hope stifled a wince and calmly finished his tie. She stepped back and pretended to objectively study his appearance. What she saw with her eyes was a strikingly handsome man. What she saw with her heart, however, was a tense, overtired man who gave two-hundred percent of himself for others, but refused to let anyone give to him. For the briefest of time that afternoon he'd relaxed, but the phone call had put an end to that.

Deciding his tie was too straight to use as an excuse to touch him, she turned away, gathering up her wrap from where she'd left it lying over the gleaming banister.

"That's the dress you wore in Paris," Tristan said behind her. "Why didn't you get something new? I thought that personal shopper was supposed to—"

"I like this dress." She had dozens of outfits now, all nipped and tucked and fitting her like she'd been born to them. She'd shopped. She'd explored the sights that San Diego had to offer. She'd expended rolls and rolls of film at the Wild Animal Park and the zoo.

She supposed it was every girl's fantasy life come true. Within the confines of his office, Tristan made a call and people came trotting over to do his bidding.

Fantasy or not, Hope knew she'd never been so alone. The phone calls she'd gotten from Justine and Gram that afternoon when Tristan had once again shut himself in his office had only underscored it.

"It does suit you."

She frowned, then realized he was still referring to her dress, and looked down at herself. "Thank you," she murmured. "Perhaps we should go? I think we're already late."

He didn't reply and Hope looked at him. His jaw ticked rhythmically. "Tristan?"

"You don't have to go tonight, you know."

"So you've already said. If you don't want me going, just say so."

"I didn't say that."

"Then what's the problem?"

He watched her for a moment, and then turned and slung his tuxedo jacket over his shoulder, heading for the interior door of the garage. "There isn't a problem," he muttered.

Hope held her breath for a moment until her stomach stopped jumping around like a bouncing ball gone mad, then followed.

They took the Porsche. Tristan left the top in place, because of her she felt certain. He wouldn't say so, of course, but he'd be aware of the time it took to put her long hair up into the twist that she'd copied from a photo in one of the hairdresser's books. That was just Tristan.

It was nearly dark by the time they arrived at the beach-front home where the party was being held. Cars lined the narrow road, but there was a valet, and Tristan left the car and keys with the young man, then escorted Hope toward the coolly modern house.

The doors were open and music blasted from inside, underscored by chatter and laughter. Tris handed over the engraved invitation, and they stepped inside. Hope swallowed the nervousness clutching her throat. She realized her fingers were clinging to his arm and carefully loosened her frantic grip. She felt his eyes on her, but kept her attention on the glittering group of people crammed into the house. And after a moment, she felt his hand at the small of her back as they entered.

After the first gala, Hope had gotten used to the vaguely shocked expressions of the people who greeted Tristan when he introduced her as his wife. She'd learned how to smile and avoid direct answers when one sleek woman after another had arched their eyebrows and asked how she'd manage to land such an elusive fish. She'd also realized, after that first gala, that Tristan was even less enamored of those public events than she.

Predictably, he was surrounded by a half-dozen people as soon as they realized he'd arrived. Hope calmly let them edge her out of the way, and started weaving in and out of people toward the buffet table she'd glimpsed.

Someone stuck a glass of champagne in her face, and she automatically took it as she looked over the sumptuous buffet. Shrimp and crab. Caviar and little golden toast points. Crudités, cheese, crackers. Chocolates, tiny cakes.

"I hope you see something to your taste."

Hope looked up, and the champagne sloshed over the edge of her glass when her hand jerked. She'd only seen the woman on the covers of fashion magazines, but Serena Stevenson was even more breathtaking in person. She blinked and looked blindly down at the buffet. It was as much a work of art in its display as anything. She picked up a napkin and dabbed the drops of alcohol from her hand. "It's magnificent."

"I'm glad you think so." The other woman smiled even more brightly, her face positively lighting up. Hope's stomach dropped, and she knew who had stepped up behind her even without that signal. She stiffened when Tristan dropped his fingers over her shoulder. "Hello, Serena. Still throwing the best parties, I see."

"Tristan, I am so glad you came. It's been too long." Serena stepped forward in a cloud of expensive perfume and reached up to kiss his cheek. Then she turned again to Hope and held out her hand, her smile seemingly genuine. "And this must be your new wife I've been hearing about. I'm very happy to meet you."

Hope shook her hand. Even in her beautiful Parisian dress, she felt like a dowdy goose next to such a graceful swan. Fortunately, Serena didn't linger.

Serena Stevenson was the hostess.

Hope set down her glass.

"Something wrong?" Tristan's lips brushed her ear again, sending shivers dancing down her spine.

He'd known they were coming to Serena's house. He'd told Hope that she didn't need to accompany him, but she hadn't taken the hint. She shook her head, not looking at him. "Noisy," she shouted.

He nodded, and she watched his eyes stray yet again to their hostess, who was circling the room like some beautiful, exotic bird.

Hope's head suddenly pounded. From the noise. From the cigarette smoke. From the sight of her husband being unable to tear his eyes away from a woman with whom he'd once been involved.

Standing in the center of the crowded room that looked as if it had come out of an architectural magazine, Serena started speaking eloquently about the efforts supporting the crisis center where she'd been helped herself as a child many years ago. And now that she'd returned to San Diego she was determined to see that others continued to be aided as she had been. And when she held out her hand and Tristan stepped forward, Hope made herself focus. Hearing just enough to know that he'd made some enormous endowment that would ensure the center would operate in the black for years to come.

All around her, people were clapping.

Nobody even noticed when Hope slipped to the back of the room and out the doors that opened onto a veranda with steps leading right down to the sand.

But even on the veranda there were people.

The urge to run down the stairs and keep on running was strong. But she kept her steps slow and measured. When she reached the sand, she removed her high-heeled pumps and started walking toward the softly crashing surf that filled the air with the pungent scent of salt water. The closer she got to the water, the darker it became away from the lights of the house. And quieter.

She reached sand that was hard packed and damp beneath her bare feet and, uncaring of the dress, she sat right down on it, folding her arms around her legs. The pain in her chest had nothing to do with her trek through the sand.

"I told you that you didn't have to come tonight."

Hope didn't look up at Tristan. A part of her was surprised that he'd followed her. But another part had been expecting him. "She's the one, isn't she?"

"The one what?"

Hope frowned, dashing a discreet hand across her cheek. A wave rolled over in a splash of foam, sending water rippling ever closer to Hope's bare feet. "The one who broke your heart."

Chapter Thirteen

Her question hung in the air.

After a long moment, Tristan lowered himself beside her and sighed grimly. "The one whose heart *I* broke," he corrected quietly.

Hope closed her eyes, turning her cheek to rest on her knees. "What happened?"

"Does it matter?"

"Everything about you matters, Tristan," she murmured tiredly. "You're the only one who doesn't realize that."

"We met after I'd started T-Comp. We became involved."

"Lovers, you mean."

"Yes." His voice was flat.

"She still cares about you." Hope had seen it in the other woman's vividly green eyes.

"She is married, Hope. Don't start looking for ghosts that don't exist. We were together a long time ago."

"And now you're back together, supporting a cause that obviously has deep meaning for her."

"I got involved with Chalmers years ago because of Serena, yes. But she moved away to New York and I stayed involved with Chalmers because I believe in the work they do. That's it. Our mutual involvement now is a coincidence. That's all."

"I don't believe you."

"I haven't made a habit of lying to you."

Hope lifted her head and pushed to her feet, brushing at her dress. "Lying to yourself is much more your forte," she said softly. "Why can't you just admit that she once meant something to you?"

He stood also and shoved Hope's pumps into his pocket. "She was beautiful, and the sex was good."

She ached inside. Not only because she could never hope to compete with a woman like Serena Stevenson, but because she felt the knot of anguish inside him like she bore it herself. He'd cared for Serena and for all Hope knew, he still did. "She's beautiful and she looks at you like a woman looks at a man for whom she cares deeply."

Even in the moonlight, Hope could see the fierce angle of his jaw. "Trust me, Hope. She knows me too well for that."

"Why?"

"Because when she lost the baby she was pregnant with—my baby—I was relieved." His words were clipped. "Relieved." He turned away.

Hope covered her mouth. Tears stung her eyes. "Oh, Tristan. I'm so sorry."

"So was she."

"You were scared."

His shoulders visibly stiffened. "I was relieved. I didn't want kids when I was twenty-two. I sure in hell don't want them now."

"But you're wonderful with them."

He snorted. "Says who?"

"I know about the volunteer work you do at Chalmers House," Hope murmured. "You give your money, certainly. But you give your time, too. I heard that you take those kids to the beach, the movies. Horseback riding. That you go by regularly, showing them how to use computers and such."

"Yeah, well, they're not *my* kids."

Hope chewed the inside of her lip and barely kept herself from placing her hand on her flat abdomen. Tristan was a man who didn't leave things to chance. He'd protected her on the flight from France, and only during the darkest hours of night would she admit that she wouldn't be upset if the condom had failed. "Just because you weren't devastated when Serena lost your baby doesn't mean you're unfeeling," she reasoned gently. "Tristan, you were young."

"The same age you are now," he pointed out abruptly. "I don't want to talk about this."

"Why not?"

"Because it doesn't serve any good purpose."

"Talking about feelings serves *every* good purpose."

"Aren't you the little expert, now."

"Have you ever talked about the baby with any-one? Even with Serena?"

"Serena knew exactly how I felt. It's why she left," he said flatly. "She wasn't even showing yet when she lost it, and she knew what kind of a man I was when I didn't share her grief."

Hope took a step nearer to him. "Why didn't you?"

"I don't want a woman having my kid. Okay?"

"Why not?" Going on instinct, she settled her hands on his chest. His heart chugged like a crazed freighter.

"Dammit, Hope—"

"Why not?" She slid her hands around his back, beneath his jacket. She felt his muscles bunch and flex. She let her body form to his unnaturally rigid stance.

He suddenly pushed her away, but his hands on her shoulders kept her from stumbling. "The night of my seventh birthday," he said flatly, "I found my father in his bedroom with one hand wrapped around a half-empty bottle of whiskey and the other holding a Smith & Wesson. Christmas Eve. He missed her so much, I think he was getting ready to eat that gun and it was my fault she was gone. She died having me," he said harshly. "Why the hell do you think I don't want children?"

"My mother died when I was two," she countered swiftly, anger hitting her sharply. For her loss. For Squire Clay's. And for Tristan, who'd been marked by the actions of a grieving man through no fault of his own. "And she *did* die by her own hand because she was so distraught that the man she loved wouldn't marry her because she had *me*. Justine told me so when I was a teenager." Hope yanked the chain out from beneath her dress and the wedding ring swung back and forth wildly. "Does that mean I should never find a man to love? To never have a child?"

"Your mother." He spoke so softly she almost didn't hear it. "I thought Gerri died in an accident," he said more naturally.

"When I asked Gram if what Justine said was true, she admitted to me that my mother drove her car head-on into an approaching semi. Gram never talks about it much, but I know she feels that she should have been able to prevent it. I never want to hurt Gram that way."

He scrubbed his hands over his face, muttering under his breath. "I'm sorry. I didn't know."

The anger left as swiftly as it had come, leaving her feeling chilled and empty. "I'm sorry for what your father went through. But you can't blame yourself for your mother's death any more than I can for mine."

"I don't—"

"Don't you? You probably blamed yourself when Serena lost your baby, too."

"Dammit, Hope, don't you get it? If I could have loved Serena, I would have. I tried and it was never there. It wasn't there with anyone."

Not even you. The words weren't said, but she heard them in his thoughts. "So you think that just because you didn't love *them,* you are incapable of loving *anyone?* That is such a cop-out."

He jerked. Stared. "What?"

"You are so intelligent." Hope couldn't stop the words once they started. "You see things around you and fix them. You try to make life better for others. You do all these wonderful things—you married me and I was weak enough to let it happen when there was probably another way to solve that problem—and you take the coward's way out by convincing yourself that it really isn't your *heart* leading you to do all this in the first place. You claim to be some sort of user. But really, you're just afraid of being hurt like all the rest of us poor souls in the world. Only you won't admit it. You hold yourself off, untouched, uninvolved emotionally because it's safer than putting yourself on the line."

Her words rang out, underscored by the steady throb of the tide. Leaving her breathless and him silent as a stone. Hope let her necklace fall back into place. "His name was Johnny Mueller," she said abruptly.

Tristan's eyes narrowed. "Who?"

"We dated in college. I thought it was love and when he, uh, didn't want to...well, you know, I thought he was being sweet and old-fashioned. Respecting me, you know." Hope looked out at the rolling ocean. It was such a magnificent sight. But it wasn't Wyoming. And she missed her home more than she could say.

She turned away and looked at Tristan. Beyond his shoulders she could see the brightly lit house. "But Johnny didn't want me. He wanted my access in the dean's office to change a failing grade to passing so he could graduate. Johnny was a user, Tristan. That's not what you are."

"A failing grade is small potatoes to things I've done."

"A person whose actions are self-serving is a user no matter what the arena. That's not who you are, Tristan. It's more a description of *me* than you."

He snorted. "You don't have a self-serving bone in your body."

"I married you."

"To save the school."

She moistened her lips. "There was probably other ways to fight Bennett. I was just too rattled to think of them. You sacrificed yourself for me. And I let you."

"Sacrifice," he repeated slowly. "Bull."

"What have you gotten out of this?"

His eyebrow lifted. "Don't underestimate yourself, Hope."

Her skin burned. She crossed her arms around herself tightly. "A few hours of sex."

"Making love."

She scrabbled for composure. "You said it wasn't."

"I lied."

Her eyes suddenly burned. She felt like a breathless racehorse chasing after that ever-elusive carrot. "Then why—" Her throat closed. She swallowed and moistened her lips. "—then why am I sleeping in one bedroom and you in another?"

The question seemed to echo again and again in her thoughts. And with each ticking second, each whoosh of the ocean, Hope knew he wasn't going to answer.

It broke her heart.

"I want to go home," she said after an eternity.

"I'll have the valet bring the car around."

"I don't mean your home, Tristan. I mean mine. I want to go home to Wyoming."

No. The response churned in Tristan's gut. He didn't know if her words were accurate or not. All he knew was he didn't like all this…emotion. It wasn't the love she deserved and he didn't like feeling churned up one bit.

"And before you take control, I'll make my own arrangements to get there," she said. "I'm a grown woman. It's time I began acting like it."

He knew good and well how grown up she was. And it was causing him no end of sleepless nights. "I never thought you weren't capable."

"I know. I was the one who thought it." Her soft lips pressed together and there was a liquid gleam in her eyes. The moonlight? Or tears? "You've helped me learn otherwise. If for nothing else, I'll always be grateful for that."

"That sounds like good-bye."

"It is."

"You're still my wife."

"On paper," she said huskily. "Not in your heart."

"I knew I'd end up hurting you."

She shook her head. "Oh, Tristan. I know I'm just a relatively inexperienced kindergarten teacher and you're a brilliant, worldly man, but even I can see the real truth. The one you're hurting is yourself."

There was an odd calmness on her face that disturbed him more than anything.

"I know what I want for my birthday," she said suddenly.

He jerked. Her birthday. Oh, hell. "It's today."

He should have remembered even though she hadn't mentioned it. It was on the birth certificate he'd gotten from Ruby, after all. The birth certificate that held nearly as many secrets as his own life held.

She smiled and it cut him deeply. Because she didn't seem to blame him for not realizing it.

"Anything," he said gruffly. "Whatever you want, it's yours."

"Go talk to Serena," Hope whispered gently. "Let go of the guilt you feel. Maybe when you do, you'll find your heart isn't as dysfunctional as you fear."

She pulled her pumps from his pocket, turned and walked away.

Tris pressed his palms against his eyes. He swore at himself. This is what happened when he didn't stick with the computers he knew.

She should have shrieked at him for being insensitive. Isn't that what all women despaired of in their men? But, *no,* she'd worried about a relationship that was dead and gone and years past. She worried about who protected *him.*

Yanking the tie loose around his neck, Tris headed toward Serena's high-priced beach house. Maybe Hope was right about that one thing, at least. It was long past time for him to make his peace with her. And once he did, he'd collect his wife and "make" something else.

Only once he returned to the house, Hope was gone.

* * *

Hope heard the door slam downstairs, but continued folding her clothing into the suitcase. She pushed a pair of rolled up socks into one of the corners and dashed her hand across her cheeks as she walked over to the closet and stared at the garments hanging inside. She'd leave the designer gowns, she decided. It wasn't as if she'd have a lot of use for them in Weaver.

But she'd take the black dress from Paris.

It was sitting on the chair by the bed. She'd put it in last because it was still slightly damp from sitting on the beach.

Only by concentrating on such details was she holding together. What she wanted to do was throw herself on the bed and weep for a week. But tears weren't the answer to the mess in her life. So why, then, did they keep leaking out the corners of her eyes, making it hard to focus on the clothing she pulled from the hangers?

She wiped her cheeks again. And pulled out her grandmother's lace dress. Hope's *wedding* dress.

Her hands trembled as she folded it. Through the closed bedroom door, she heard Tristan's distinctive footsteps on the stairs.

The door slammed open and she whirled around, her hands clenching around the dress.

Tristan stood there, his hair looking as if it had been combed by a whirlwind and his tie hanging loose about his unbuttoned collar. The sleeves of his shirt were rolled haphazardly up his forearms and his hands were curled into fists. ''You're so anxious to go home that you can't even wait for me at the party? Proving your independence is that important?'' He advanced into the room. ''I thought you went back to the house,'' he gritted. ''I looked for you for nearly an hour in that crowd. I had nightmares of you doing something crazy, of hitching a ride or falling for some stranger's line. And then I find out that you got the car from the valet.''

''I'm not a fool!''

''I know you're not,'' he snapped. ''You're a beautiful woman who was upset.''

''What did you think I'd do? Take your Porsche and drive it into a semi like my mother did?''

He sighed noisily and shoved his hands through his hair. ''How do you know that's what your... what Gerri did? That it was deliberate?''

''I told you. Justine told me.'' She refolded the dress and put it in the nearly full suitcase, then tightened the belt of her robe.

''How often do you talk to her?''

''She called today to tell me happy birthday. Why?''

His shoulders seemed to sag for a moment. Hope could feel his distress like a tangible thing. She wanted to ease it for him more than anything. But she couldn't.

She turned to the suitcase and folded the flap in place, zipping it shut.

''I don't want you to go.''

Her lips parted. She braced her hands on either side of the suitcase and closed her eyes for a brief moment. There was no point to the crying relief that his words brought. It wasn't as if he'd professed undying devotion. ''I'll have to sooner or later,'' she said once she was sure her voice wouldn't fail. "That was the intention all along."

"Then go later."

Hope straightened. "Why? Why do you say this now?" She knew she sounded frustrated and hurt, but she couldn't help it. "You don't just change your mind in the middle of the stream, Tristan. You never wanted a wife."

"I never said that."

"You didn't have to. You needn't worry about protecting my reputation any longer. You shouldn't have had to worry about it in the first place."

"I like having you around."

She flipped her hair behind her back and swallowed the fresh pain of that. "Sort of like a pet you're fond of?" she said flippantly.

"Dammit, Hope." His lips thinned. "What do you want me to say?"

That you care for me! If only a little. "Nothing. I just want to go home. Where I belong. My world is Weaver. Your world is…the rest of the world." She pulled the suitcase off the bed, staggering a step under the weight of it. She lugged it past Tristan into the hall, propped it, angled, on the steps and followed it as it practically pulled her down the stairs with it.

She left it by the front door. She'd arranged for a shuttle to pick her up at six in the morning and take her to the airport. It wasn't as stylish a method as Tristan might have used, but it would work just fine for her.

Painfully aware of Tristan descending the stairs, she turned and went into the great room. She should have known he'd follow. Maybe she did know. Maybe she was aching for a confrontation. Something. Anything to expend the tangle of emotions churning inside her.

He entered the room and turned on a lamp. "We didn't have to get married in order to stop the school board from charging you with moral misconduct."

"I know. I should have fought Bennett right from the beginning. Instead, I just let it all happen right around us."

"No." He held out a cream-colored piece of paper. "You only needed this."

"What is it?"

"Your birth certificate. You've never seen it, have you? Every time you had to present it for some reason, your grandmother was with you. She handled the paperwork for you." It wasn't really a question. More an observation.

She frowned, looking at the square document. "Well, yes. I guess so. I never thought about it. You probably got it from Gram for the passport. How did you get that processed so quickly, anyway?"

"Look at it."

She didn't want to. She knew it was silly. But she really, truly didn't want to touch it. Not when he looked so grim. "What? I'm adopted or something?" she joked shakily. "That's why I didn't inherit the Leoni looks?"

He held out the paper.

She swallowed and took it in her hand, but still didn't look. Long ago she'd asked Ruby about her father, but Ruby had become so distressed, Hope had never asked again. She'd never been able to stand upsetting Gram. Feeling her pulse beating inside her head, Hope looked down at the document. There it was. The name of her father.

She couldn't breathe. "No. No, it's not possible." She looked up at Tristan. His eyes were filled with regret. *"Bennett?"*

Tristan nodded.

Hope grappled with the fact. "What did he have in common with my mother? Wouldn't he have been in college? My mother was older—" she broke off. Tristan's expression was even more gentle. And suddenly, Hope knew. She *knew.*

She looked at the document again and there, in the place where it should have said Geraldine Leoni, it had another name entirely. "Justine," Hope whispered.

The birth certificate fluttered from her fingers to the carpet.

Tristan caught her as her knees gave way, and carried her to the couch.

Chapter Fourteen

"I don't know why I'm crying," Hope said thickly a long while later.

"You've had a shock," Tris murmured. He ran his hand down her glossy hair. His shirt front was wet from her tears. Her nose was red, and her eyes were puffy. She was so damned beautiful it made him ache inside.

"I can't believe this is happening. That I didn't know. How could I have been so blind? So stupid?"

"Whoa." He put his thumb under her chin and lifted her face. "How were you supposed to know?"

Her eyes, drowning pools of purple, were beyond pain. "I feel like a fool. Who hasn't looked at their own birth certificate?"

"Someone who's never been given the opportunity to," he reasoned. "I don't think I saw my own until I had to replace my social security card when I was in college. Justine was only sixteen when you were born in Colorado. Gerri and Ruby were only trying to protect both of you.''

"But Justine—God, my mother. We talk maybe three, four times a year. She's practically a stranger to me. She must hate the sight of me."

"I doubt that." He pressed his lips to her temple.

"Then why did they lie all these years? Why didn't Gram tell Bennett to lay off?"

"Ruby's managed to keep everyone in town from needing to see your birth certificate. Probably wasn't hard. Weaver is a small place—they don't usually need that type of ID. Ruby said Bennett doesn't know."

Hope laughed brokenly. "How pathetic. He'd just croak knowing that he is my…my—"

Tris brushed his thumb over her lips. "He'd be proud if he's got any sense at all. There's no love lost between his family and mine, but he's not stupid." He smiled faintly. "What may give him a coronary, actually, is knowing that his daughter is a Clay by marriage."

Hope's eyes crinkled with humor for a second, but then they filled again. She shifted and pushed herself out of his arms. "So you married me for nothing, after all. All I'd have had to do was tell my, uh, Bennett, that the girl he was trying to tar and feather was his own flesh and blood and he'd have ceased and desisted."

"Presumably. But Ruby didn't want you to find out like that."

"She didn't want me to find out at all! How could

she lie to me all these years? Keep this from me? I'd have surely found out eventually.''

"She loves you. People do odd things all the time in the name of love.''

Hope's face crumpled. "I know. God, I know. Gram's been everything to me. I'm the first one in her family who finished college, did you know that? She was so proud. What am I going to say to her? What will I say to Bennett? And Justine. Poor Justine. She must have been so scared.''

"Say whatever you want to say. It's your call, sweet pea.''

Hope pushed from the couch, rubbing her hands over her cheeks. "Why did you tell me this, now?''

He should have known her mind would insist on seeing all the angles. "To prove that marrying you wasn't the only option. It was just the one I preferred. So don't go around thinking that I made some ultimate sacrifice. I warned you I was a selfish soul.''

Her eyebrows pulled together. "But…but, why?''

"Because I liked being with you," he admitted abruptly. "And I don't want you to leave, now.''

"Did you talk to Serena?''

His jaw tightened. "Yes. She *is* happy, Hope. Happier than she ever was with me. And no matter what you think, it is long over between us.''

"If…if I do stay, what, um—''

"It'll be in my bedroom," he finished bluntly. "I want you in my bed, Hope. There's no point in pretending it ain't so. Tried that. Didn't work.''

"I still have to go home to Weaver. School starts in about six weeks.''

He didn't like acknowledging it, but it was staring him in the face. "You really miss it there, don't you? That painting—it reminds you of home."

She was running her fingers along the necklace in that old, nervous habit of hers. "I do miss it. I miss Gram." Her eyes shut, and Tris saw a tear slip down her cheek. "What am I supposed to do now, Tristan? Where do we go from here?"

Tris wished he had an answer. He stood and went over to her, tilting her face toward his. "It's been a helluva birthday," he murmured.

Her hands settled on his chest, fingers tangling in the fabric. "You gave me a gift no one else did," she whispered. "The truth."

"I never wanted to hurt you."

"I know. It's not in your nature to hurt people."

He had to smile. "No matter how much evidence to the contrary, you're insistent on that point, aren't you?"

She slipped her fingertips inside his shirt, touching his chest. The exact spot where his heart thudded, slow and heavy. "Your heart functions just fine," she said softly. "Thank you for being honest." She leaned up against him and brushed her lips against his.

It took every bit of control he had to keep his hands light on her waist. "Will you stay?"

She sighed. Pressed her forehead against his chin. "For a while."

Hearing it, the knot of tension in his stomach eased. He slid his arms around her, swept her into his arms, and carried her slowly up the stairs to his bedroom.

This time, when he settled her in the middle of his bed and she held out her hand to him, he didn't ignore it. He put his hand in hers, and lowered himself beside her. She lifted the necklace over her head and let it go, to puddle on the nightstand. Next, she unbuttoned his shirt, slowly tugging it from his shoulders.

Her teeth sank into the tip of her tongue and he shook his head at that, kissing her, tasting her. He spread the lapels of her soft robe, discovering her all over again. The sleek shoulders, the satin-smooth ridge of her collarbone. The dip of her waist and the crests of her beautiful breasts. The ticklish spot on the arch of her foot and the sweet heat between her legs.

Her hands tangled in his hair and her legs, smooth as anything he'd ever felt in his life, tangled with his. She slid over him, her fragrant hair surrounding them. And her mouth...

"You're killing me," he finally groaned through gritted teeth and smoothly flipped her onto her back. His hands held hers over her head and he kissed her, swallowing her breathless laughter. Still holding her hands safely, he pressed into her, watching her eyes go wide, then slowly close on a long sigh of pleasure.

He let go of her hands and she touched his face with gentle fingertips, murmuring his name. Tris pressed his lips against her palm and felt his soul ache when she opened her eyes again and he saw a tear slip free. "Don't," he whispered against her lips. He pulled her close, unable to pull himself from the haven of her body, unable to bear the thought of her crying. "Don't cry."

She wound her arms around his shoulders and opened her mouth beneath his. Her knees brushed his hips and she moved, drawing him ever deeper, ever closer. Her neck arched back, luring his lips. "Don't stop," she moaned.

He felt her trembling. Felt her tension. Felt it, shared it, experienced it. He couldn't stop. Not now. Maybe not ever.

She shuddered and quaked, and Tris couldn't think anymore. He could only feel. Only hang on to the one woman who'd ever made him hope for more.

Her breath rasped in his ear. "I love you, Tristan. I love you. Now. Now."

His jaw locked. Her hips cradled his. He closed his eyes and gave himself over to the passion he could no longer contain. *Now.*

The winter landscape sat propped on top of his dresser. She'd moved it there two weeks ago when she'd moved into his bedroom. Every morning, they wakened to the sight of that small, exquisite painting.

And Tris knew their time was nearing an end. He couldn't imagine moving back to Weaver and she couldn't remain away.

She'd talked to Ruby, he knew.

Her grandmother, probably relieved that the truth was finally coming out, had finally explained what had happened when Justine found herself pregnant and just sixteen years old. Gerri had gone to Ben-

nett's parents, who'd been scandalized by the whole
thing. They'd sold their struggling ranch to the Double-C and tried to pay off Gerri to take Justine away
and never return. To her credit, Gerri had refused
the money, but they had still left town. They'd gone
to Colorado where Gerri had an old friend, and when
Hope was born, Gerri raised her as her own, since
Justine was so young and still behaving irresponsi-
bly. After a year and a half, after all the struggling
to keep her family together on a limited means,
Gerri had thought things were on the upswing when
she'd met a new man she'd been crazy about. But
it hadn't worked out when he'd learned that Gerri
never intended to give up raising her new little
granddaughter.

Ruby insisted that Gerri's accident may have been
just that. An accident. But they'd never know for
certain. And Justine, feeling guilt over the entire ep-
isode, had pleaded with Ruby to continue upholding
the lie that Hope was Gerri's daughter. She wanted
Hope to have *some* stability, and the only chance of
that would be if Ruby took her back to Weaver to
live with her.

In that, at least, Justine had been correct. Because,
aside from Ruby's strictness, she couldn't have possibly loved Hope more.

But Hope hadn't spoken with Justine.

Tris figured that might take a while. But it would
come. Of that there was no doubt. Because no one
had a greater capacity for love and forgiveness than
did Hope Leoni Clay.

As for Bennett, Tris wasn't sure how Hope felt.
She hadn't said, and he hadn't asked. If he could

have solved that problem for her, he would have. But it was something she'd have to decide herself. He had complete confidence that, whatever she did, it would be right.

The fall session at Weaver Elementary was getting closer with every day. And the hotter it became in San Diego as August neared, the more he saw her eyes lingering on that winter landscape.

Cole called him for a new job, and Tris did the unthinkable. He told his boss about his marriage, and he turned the job down. He was in the middle of programming a new video game, and Hope had been helping him with the story behind the action.

In truth, he knew he didn't want to go away just yet. There'd be time enough later. When Hope was no longer with him. When his home was just a house once again. When he was alone. Burying his attention in the bowels of a computer system was a sure-fire way of forgetting that regrettable reality.

The day he wakened and the painting was gone from his dresser, he knew. Hope was leaving. She was going home.

He found her downstairs in the kitchen. Wearing one of his button-down white shirts. The sexiest attire he could imagine her wearing. He stood in the doorway for a long while, watching her move around the kitchen. Even though it was only seven in the morning, there was already a loaf of bread cooling on a bread rack.

Then she looked over her shoulder at him and her lips curved. "Good morning," she greeted. "I thought you'd sleep for hours yet."

"Because a certain violet-eyed temptress kept me awake until the wee hours, you mean?"

Her eyes flickered and pink rose in her cheeks. She turned back to the sink and ran the towel in her hand over and around the fixtures until they gleamed. "I called Gram," she said after a moment.

Tris tucked his thumbs in his beltloops and leaned his shoulder against the doorjamb. "You can take the jet."

She gave him a startled look, then her lips twisted wryly. Sadly. "Do you really read minds," she asked curiously, "or am I just that obvious?"

"There's nothing obvious about you, Hope."

She just gave a little shake of her head, making her toffee waves ripple over her shoulders. "Oh, I think I'm utterly predictable," she murmured so softly he barely heard. "You had a call again this morning from Coleman Black."

Tris pursed his lips. "I turned him down already."

"He said to tell you it was urgent."

"With Cole it always is."

"You should call him." Her eyes drifted to the video game that he'd finally shouldered out of the middle of the kitchen. It now sat against the wall where an empty china hutch had once sat, but was now doing duty as a toy bin at Chalmers House. "Your video games are great fun. But your real interest is the work you do with Cole." Work that he'd finally opened up about and shared fully with her.

"For a woman still wet behind the ears, you're awful full of insight." His tone was teasing.

"I dried behind them this morning," she replied lightly. Then she folded the dish towel and set it on the counter with an air of finality. "Tristan—"

"Don't. Your life is there. Mine isn't. We both know it."

She moistened her lips and smiled. Bittersweet. He saw her twist the rings on her finger. "What about, um—"

"You're my wife, Hope. Together or not, I don't see any reason to change that."

"You might change your mind."

"You might find someone who loves you the way you should be loved."

Her eyes closed for a moment. Her long, lovely throat worked. "Well. I guess I should get dressed. Gram is expecting me before evening."

He could talk her into staying. He knew he could. But every day she'd look at that wintry landscape and wish for Weaver. It would kill him. "I'll drive you to the airport."

Her eyes glistened. "I've arranged a driver," she said huskily. "It's better this way."

Nothing was better. But he nodded anyway, because he could see she needed to do this her way. She passed by him, and he breathed in the scent of her, holding it in his mind. Wondering how long it would be before he forgot it.

Shoving his hands through his hair, he walked through the house, seeing the little signs of Hope everywhere. The jar in the foyer filled with wild-flowers she'd picked when she'd talked him into renting horses at the nearby stable. The charcoal drawing of her from Paris, that was such a perfect rendition of the tentative confidence she'd been gaining there, hung on the wall near his office. The oversized paperback book she'd left on the cocktail table in the great room. She'd been studying science project ideas geared toward the primary grades.

Turning his back on it all, he went into his office and closed the door. He didn't go out again until he heard the doorbell chime and knew that the driver had come to collect Hope.

She wore a lilac-colored sheath that ended just above her knees and left her arms bare. Her hair was pulled back in a gold clip. She looked cool and chic and lovely and totally capable of handling anything the world tossed her way.

Including a husband who didn't have the guts to reach out for the love she so freely offered.

Hope looked at Tristan, determined not to break down. She knew she had to leave. Her kids depended on her. Gram needed her. But most of all, it was time for her handsome husband to move out of the limbo in which they'd been tentatively existing. "I do love you." The words came out, even though she'd been determined not to say them again.

His eyes were so darkly blue they looked nearly black. "Call me when you get there."

She nodded, even though she knew she wouldn't. The next move had to be his. "Think Gram will recognize me?" she asked.

He didn't smile. "Your violet eyes will give you away."

She reached for the door. Her cases had already been carried out to the waiting limousine. "Well..."

Suddenly he was next to her, hauling her against

him. Her mouth opened under his and her bones dissolved. She kissed him with all the love in her heart. All the love she prayed was in his.

When he finally lowered her toes back to the tile floor, Hope's eyes were burning. But she couldn't go without touching his ruggedly beautiful face once more. She drew her fingertip along his tight jaw. And prayed with everything inside her that her husband would find his way from the cocoon just the way she had. "Good-bye, Tristan."

She pulled open the door and stepped outside.

The sun was just starting to burn through the morning fog. It would be a hot August day.

The limousine was on the street, aligned perfectly with the brick walkway. The rear door was open and waiting.

She held her shoulders straight. And walked toward the vehicle. She didn't look back.

Chapter Fifteen

Tris stared at the little package in the drawer of the bathroom cabinet. A home pregnancy test.

He couldn't breathe. He yanked open the bottom cupboard door and fumbled with the small trash can, pulling it out and rummaging through it until he found the little white stick.

He closed his eyes, slid down to the floor and wondered if he had the nerve to look.

It had been two weeks since Hope walked out of his California house. Two weeks of being unable to sleep in his own bed, instead taking refuge in the room she'd used that first week. The room attached to this very bathroom. Two weeks since he'd answered his phone, checked his e-mail, left the house.

It wasn't pleasant to know he was such a coward. But he realized he didn't know what cowardice was until he sat there, afraid to see what that little white stick showed.

He wished he had a drink. But he'd realized the first week after Hope left that he couldn't live his life in a bottle. It reminded him too much of the night he'd come across Squire.

He stared at himself in the mirror. He looked like hell. He felt worse. Swearing under his breath, he tipped the pregnancy test stick into his hand and turned it over.

Stared. Stared while his muscles went lax and his brain seemed to explode in his head. Stared while it felt as if his chest would crack open from the ache that expanded and multiplied.

His hands shook so badly that the little white stick tumbled to the floor. Face up where he could still see the results.

God.

Tris let out a low groan. Oh, God. Did anything ever hurt so badly? His eyes burned, his vision blurred. Dammit, dammit, dammit. He pressed the heels of his palms against his eyes.

He was such a bloody fool.

He wasn't sure how long he sat there. His knees were stiff and his head ached when he finally pushed to his feet and went into his room. The room he hadn't entered since the day Hope left.

But the shocks of the day weren't over. For on the nightstand, he caught the glint of gold.

Her necklace. With the ring that she'd worn since she was twelve. Tris sank on the edge of the bed and picked up the ring. Despite the burning in his eyes, he turned it, noticing the inscription that hadn't been there before. He tilted it to the light.

You are my heart.

His gut ached, and he knew she'd left the ring for him. That she'd had it inscribed for him. He let out a long, hard breath.

He picked up the phone and started punching numbers. Thirty minutes later, he was in the air, knowing he could clean up on the plane. A chartered chopper was waiting for him when they landed in Gillette, and it took him straight to the Double-C.

The arrival of a helicopter wasn't exactly everyday fare and Tris wasn't surprised to find he had a landing party when he climbed out and gave a thumbs-up to the pilot. The chopper took off once more, and Tris turned to see Squire and Matthew standing there.

"You all right?" Matthew asked.

Tris nodded. Satisfied, Matthew turned and headed for the horse that was ground-tied a safe distance away from where the chopper had landed. Which just left Squire. Tris looked at his old man. "How's married life?"

Squire lifted an eyebrow. "You tell me."

"It's gonna get better," Tris said abruptly. "I've come to get the cameo."

"The one she wore when we got hitched."

Tris nodded. "Yes."

"To give to Hope. It's about time. Your mama would have approved of your choice, boy." Squire slanted a look his way. "Even if she wouldn't have approved of letting your bride come home all by herself for days on end. We've all been making a point of checking on your new bride.''

Tris barely kept himself from rolling his shoulders against the itch that accompanied the censure from his old man. ''I don't think my mother would have approved of you holding a gun to your head on my seventh birthday, either.''

Squire stopped so short, the gravel beneath his boots kicked up a pile of dust. ''What?''

Tris hadn't planned to say that. He also hadn't planned to fall for a woman who was eleven years younger than he was. He hadn't planned a lot of things. ''Christmas Eve. My seventh birthday. You were in your room. You had a bottle of whiskey in one hand and your gun in another.''

Squire settled his gray Stetson more firmly on his head. ''In my hand, son. Not against my head.''

''You weren't thinking about ending it all then? You weren't missing your wife so damned bad that it was almost worth giving in to the pain? You were alone for thirty-four years, Squire. Because I was born.'' The memory of that long-ago day was so clear in Tristan's mind it was as if he hadn't spent all the years since, trying to ignore its existence. His father, who'd made a life out of being unemotional and hard-edged, had had a single track of tears running down his lean, tanned face. ''You told me you were cleaning the gun and sent me back to bed,'' he remembered.

Squire sighed. ''There's a lotta years under that bridge, boy. I remember that night, though. Seemed like the years of missing her sleeping next to me all rolled up together, damned near drowning me in misery. Or mebbe it was the whiskey that was drowning me. But it was my son with his mother's eyes who saved me. Come on. I got something to give you. Besides the cameo.''

Curbing his impatience, Tris followed Squire into the house. They entered through the mudroom in the rear, where the wooden screen door squeaked and slapped shut the way it always had. It was the sound of his childhood, he thought. Squire headed back through the house to the spacious room beyond the wide staircase that he now shared with his new wife. Squire went to the closet and rummaged around one of the shelves, and returned with a hank of white fabric bunched in his hand.

''Your mama was a stubborn woman,'' he said. ''I was mighty mad at her for dying. But more mad at myself because if I had insisted she stay inside instead of going out to the old barn, or if I'd just gone out there for her in the first place, she wouldn't have been out in that snowstorm. She wouldn't have slipped and fallen. It was my fault, pure and simple. And it's only because of Gloria that I've learned to live with it.''

It was more information than Squire had ever offered about the night of his mother's death. ''What was she looking for in the barn?''

''A Christmas present she'd made.'' Squire held up the fabric that he'd retrieved. ''This.''

Tris realized it was a small dress. Sized for an infant.

''It's a baptism gown,'' Squire said. ''For you. She wanted you, Tristan. She wanted all you boys. Don't ever doubt that she'd have changed one thing in her life.'' He handed the small white garment to Tris. ''Think she'd like the idea of your Hope having this, as well as the cameo.''

Your Hope. That's exactly what she was. His hope. For happiness for the future. For a life that wasn't centered around microchips, processors and cables.

His throat tight, Tris managed a grin. ''So, Pop, can I borrow the keys to the car?''

''Could I get a cup?'' Tristan flipped over the down-turned coffee cup in front of where he sat at the counter. Hope swallowed her shock and forced herself to walk across the café to the front door and pull it closed. The air conditioner hummed and she could already feel cool air flowing. ''We're closed in the afternoons,'' she said.

His lips curved enticingly. ''Just one cup?''

She wanted to throttle him. She wanted to put her arms around him and kiss his beautiful, hard face. She rounded the counter and grabbed up the coffee pot. It was cold, but she poured it in his cup anyway.

''Not going to spill this time, huh?''

She clasped her hands together atop the counter. ''No.''

''Good.'' He shifted, then set a folded bunch of fabric on the counter. ''You know, I don't remember what happened to that gray sweater I wore that first day.''

Hope felt her cheeks flush. She'd been sleeping in that sweater every night since she'd left California. Her electricity bill had doubled because she'd been running the air conditioner just so she'd still be comfortable enough to sleep. "It's around some-where, I'm sure. I'll have to look for it," she mur-mured. Then moistened her lips nervously when he slid one of his hands over hers. Under. Palm meeting palm.

His eyes, those intense sapphire eyes watched her. It was as bad as that first day. No, worse. She could hear her pulse, thundering in her ears. Could hear her breath, slowly easing past her lips. She could hear the soft chink of his gold wristwatch as it bumped the counter beneath their hands.

"Relax," he said in that voice that hypnotized. His thumb swirled over her hand. "It was just a sweater."

She realized she was leaning toward him and straightened like a shot, pulling her hands away from his. "What are you doing here?"

He smiled slightly and lifted the coffee cup, drinking slowly as if it were the best coffee in the world and not a good three hours old and stone cold. "Not exactly a glowing welcome," he said.

She couldn't smile and joke. Not now. Not any-more. "I'm not pregnant," she said baldly. And she'd cried for a solid day when she'd learned it. She'd left California the next day. "If that's what's worrying you, you can stop."

He set aside the cup and slowly laid a familiar-looking white stick on the counter. "I know. I never knew how much I would regret that until I found this," he replied, his voice low.

"Tristan."

"No. I need to tell you." His jaw cocked. "I

found this, and I wished it had been positive. That you'd been pregnant.''

His gaze met hers. His eyes were so filled with grief that her heart clenched. ''I started out thinking I could satisfy myself with just a kiss from you,'' he said gruffly. ''One kiss. But a kiss doesn't begin to cover it. I want you to have my baby, Hope.''

Hope saw the ravages in his eyes. Her heart squeezed. ''Oh, Tristan.''

He slid the bundle of fabric in front of her and spread it out. ''My mother made this,'' he said roughly. ''For me, apparently. But obviously, I've outgrown it a size or two. So if we're gonna get any use out of it, we'll have to start with something less than six-five.''

Hope looked at the delicate tucks and fine stitching of the white gown. She was afraid to hope.

''It's a baptism dress,'' he said. ''You're not pregnant yet, so we'll just have to keep trying.''

Her teeth worried her inner lip. ''Are you sure?''

His lips twisted. ''I'm not saying it'll be the most peaceful nine months of my life, but if you're willing to give it a go, I'm your man.''

She touched the dress, her fingers trembling. He couldn't mean it.

''Tell me why you wanted to make love that day on the flight back from France.''

''Because I loved you,'' she said. ''And I knew you didn't want to hear those words from me.''

''I did. I wanted to hear them. Even when I couldn't acknowledge the stuff inside me, I wanted them from you.''

Her heart thundered. ''What do you want now?''

"Let me back in your life, Hope. Nothing's been right since you left."

Hope trembled. "Why?"

"Because you pick up where I leave off. Because you remind me that life is more than a computer cable and an uplink. Because you see inside me and have the guts to keep standing right there beside me, despite it all."

He reached over the counter and caught her left hand in his, dropping something in her palm. She looked at it. The wedding ring she'd worn around her neck since she was twelve. She let out a ragged sigh.

"Because I love you," he said softly. "And you know it's true because I've never said it before. Not even to my favorite laptop." He held out his hand. "Marry me."

Hope laughed brokenly. "I already did," she said and pushed the ring onto his finger. "It fits," she whispered.

"Perfectly." His gaze touched on her lips, and then he was folding her hands in his, tugging her close until their lips were only inches apart above the counter that still separated them. "I'll try to cut down on the traveling for Cole," he murmured. "And keep the Paris jaunts to the summertime so you can come with me."

Hope could barely breathe. She pulled back far enough to see his eyes. "Are you sure?"

"I've broken rules in the past, Hope. Maybe if you and I prove that an agent for Hollins-Winword can be happily married, Cole will finally bite the bullet and put Dom out of her misery, too."

Her lips parted. He was serious. Well and truly serious. "Where will we live?"

He smiled slowly. Stealing her breath and her heart all over again. "Here in Weaver, of course. I can't possibly take you away from your students. They're sort of responsible for bringing us together."

"But you don't like living here."

"You pointed out yourself not so long ago that I'd never *lived* here. Not really. And besides, I'm thinking of starting up another company—video games are a real hoot. I'll need an office—probably have to get that built since there's not a lot of buildings here going empty. And some employees. Might mean some new people moving to town. I've got a lot of new scenarios in mind for the programs. But I'm thinking some of the stories behind the action aren't quite right, so I might need some help in that area from an expert in that age of kids—"

"What about your house in San Diego?"

"I donated it to Chalmers House," he said. "Serena's husband is handling it, actually. He's in real estate."

Hope leaned over and kissed him. She felt his lips smile against hers. Then he was lifting her right across the counter, knocking his coffee cup sideways where it spilled. She laughed. And cried. And wrapped her arms around him, loving him more than life itself.

He lifted her hand and pressed a kiss to the rings around her finger. "I love you, Hope Leoni."

"Hope Leoni Clay." She picked up the baptism

gown and held it against her heart. "And I love you."

He smiled into her eyes, and then pulled out a lovely cameo of ivory and the palest of pink. "My mother wore this when she married the old man," he said. "She died too early but he never stopped loving her. Not even now, even though he's finally moving on with his life with Gloria." He pinned it to Hope's collar. "That's how I love you, Hope. Now. Always."

"Oh, Tristan," she whispered. She touched his jaw. A shock of brilliant gold hair had tumbled over his forehead. He was beautiful on the outside. But it was the complicated man inside that held her heart. "You are my dream come true."

His lips lowered over hers. "More than a dream," he amended. "It's hope. Hope, sweet pea. And with you by my side, I'll never lose that again."

Epilogue

A breeze drifted over the land, bringing with it the scent of alfalfa, of horses and cattle and the wide, wide open sky.

For the assembly of individuals crowded around the beribboned bassinet that sat in the sparse shade of a trio of cottonwoods, the breeze brought the scent of peace. Most of them were Clays. But there were a few others. Ruby Leoni for one. And Justine Leoni and Bennett Ludlow who were both keeping a fair distance from one another, but who were behaving for the sake of the daughter and grandson they now openly shared.

Squire Clay looked off to one side of his property. From where he stood, he could see the stand of trees that surrounded the swimming hole his grandchildren used every chance they got. The other direction, too far off for him to see, was the ranch his middle son had bought. Jefferson raised horses. Went his own way, the way he'd always done. But he and Emily and their young 'uns were close enough to home to satisfy Squire.

Matthew had never strayed far. He figured he'd brought enough of the city to the ranch when he'd married Jaimie, and Squire suspected it was so. Nobody had more zest for life than Jaimie, except maybe Matt and Jaimie's two kids.

Daniel was happy as a pup in clover with Maggie and their three. When he wasn't busy with ranch business, he was wearing a hard hat in town overseeing the construction of the new office complex that would house Tristan's new business, as well as an honest-to-God hospital. Only eighteen beds, but it was more than Squire had ever expected he'd live long enough to see. And it was needed, considering the influx of people his son's business was bringing about.

He heard wheels crunching over gravel and turned to see a sport utility vehicle bearing "Sheriff" on the side roll to a stop. The doors opened and Sawyer, his oldest, stepped out, sketching a faint wave before he went around to help his wife out of the seat. Rebecca was so big with the baby she was pregnant with, it was a wonder she didn't just tip over. But even if she did, Sawyer and Ryan were constantly hovering. They'd catch her.

Squire glanced up to the sky. It was the same color as Sarah's eyes had been—the woman who had borne him these five sons who were better men than he'd ever hoped for. Than he'd had a right to expect considering all the things he'd done wrong.

He closed his eyes for a moment, breathing in the smell of this land that had been his life for damned near all of it. When he opened them, he knew who stood beside him. Gloria. His love. The last one he'd have.

He put his arm over her shoulder and marveled again at how well she fit him. They'd been married just over two years and he still had to shake himself every morning to remind himself it was real. "Is the preacher here yet?"

Gloria shook her head. "Not yet. But he will be. He's baptized all the grandchildren. Hope's and Tristan's first won't be one he'll miss."

Her auburn head tilted and she looked at him with her lovely eyes. "Sarah's watching over all this, I think. Think she's satisfied?" Understanding shined in Gloria's eyes. Understanding of the losses and blessings, the pain and the love that all added together to form one person's life.

"I think she'd say everything was just right." He settled his gaze on Gloria. She was the one who'd opened his heart again. "The men of the Double-C have exactly what she wanted for us all along."

Gloria smiled. "Love," she finished.

"Yes, ma'am," Squire said contentedly. "Yes, indeed."

* * * * *

MAITLAND MATERNITY

Where the luckiest babies are born!

Join Harlequin® and Silhouette® for a special 12-book series about the world-renowned Maitland Maternity Clinic, owned and operated by the prominent Maitland family of Austin, Texas, where romances are born, secrets are revealed…and bundles of joy are delivered!

Look for

MAITLAND MATERNITY

titles at your favorite retail outlet, starting in August 2000

HARLEQUIN®
Makes any time special ™

Silhouette®
Where love comes alive ™

Silhouette®

SPECIAL EDITION®

COMING NEXT MONTH

#1339 WHEN BABY WAS BORN—Jodi O'Donnell
That's My Baby!

Sara was about to give birth—and couldn't remember anything except her name! But a twist of fate brought Cade McGivern to her in her moment of need, and she couldn't imagine letting this unforgettable cowboy go. Still, until she remembered everything, Sara and Cade's future was as uncertain as her past....

#1340 IN SEARCH OF DREAMS—Ginna Gray
A Family Bond

On a quest to find his long-lost brother, reporter J. T. Conway lost his heart to headstrong Kate Mahoney. But with her scandalous past, Kate wasn't welcoming newcomers. Could J.T. help Kate heal—and convince her his love was for real?

#1341 WHEN LOVE WALKS IN—Suzanne Carey

After seventeen years, Danny Finn came back, and Cate Anderson ached for the passion they'd shared as teenage sweethearts. But Danny never knew that Cate's teenage son was actually his child. Cate hadn't wanted to hurt Danny and her son with the truth. But now she and Danny were falling in love all over again....

#1342 BECAUSE OF THE TWINS...—Carole Halston

Graham Knight was surprised to learn that he was the father of twins! Luckily, pretty Holly Beaumont lent a hand with the rambunctious tots. But Graham was wary of the emotions Holly stirred within him. For he'd learned the hard way that he couldn't trust his instincts about women. Or could he...?

#1343 TEXAS ROYALTY—Jean Brashear

Private investigator Devlin Marlowe's case led him to Lacey DeMille, the Texas society girl this former rebel fell for and was betrayed by as a teenager. Now he had the opportunity for the perfect revenge. But he never counted on rekindling his desire for the only woman who had ever mattered.

#1344 LOST-AND-FOUND GROOM—Patricia McLinn
A Place Called Home

When Daniel Delligatti found Kendra Jenner and insisted on being a part of his son's life, Kendra was not pleased. After all, Daniel was a risk-taker and Kendra played by the rules. Could these opposites find common ground...and surrender to their irresistible attraction?

CMN0700